"So you won't give me a chance!"

Gina fought to keep her voice steady, fought to meet Grady's eyes without flinching.

"I'm giving you the same chance you gave our marriage, Gina." A nerve twitched alongside his strong jaw. "The same chance you gave *us*. And now, you have approximately five minutes before you're to report to the lounge. We're going to discuss various prefire plans and we'd all be fascinated by a contribution from you."

Her delicate brow furrowed. "What do you mean?"

"You trained in San Francisco. Maybe there's something you can teach us," he muttered sarcastically.

"Grady . . . ." Her eyes pleaded for understanding.

"Captain Simpson to you, *Ms Lindsay*."

It shouldn't have hurt, but it did. . . .

Rebecca Winters, an American writer and mother of four, is a graduate of the University of Utah who has also studied overseas at Swiss and French schools, including the Sorbonne. She's currently teaching French and Spanish to elementary school students. *Fully Involved* is Rebecca's second Harlequin Romance—and she's already working on her next!

Books by Rebecca Winters

HARLEQUIN ROMANCE
2953—BLIND TO LOVE

Fully Involved

Rebecca Winters

Harlequin Books

TORONTO • NEW YORK • LONDON
AMSTERDAM • PARIS • SYDNEY • HAMBURG
STOCKHOLM • ATHENS • TOKYO • MILAN

ISBN 0-373-03047-9

Harlequin Romance first edition April 1990

To Jill, Captain Gardner
and the crew at Engine 4
for their invaluable assistance

CHAPTER ONE

"CAPTAIN SIMPSON? Regina Lindsay reporting for duty." She checked her gold watch nervously and noted with satisfaction that there were still two minutes to go until the new shift took over. After all her planning, she couldn't afford to make any mistakes now.

The smell of frying bacon from the interior of the station reached her nostrils, making her feel slightly nauseated. She hadn't slept well, anticipating this moment, and couldn't eat breakfast. Her emotions were tying her in knots.

The darkly attractive man seated at the desk put down the copy of *Fire Command* he'd been reading and lifted his head. He was wearing his luxuriant black hair shorter than she remembered. In his days as a newspaper foreign correspondent, he rarely found the time to get it cut. She'd always liked his hair longer because it had a tendency to curl, reminding her of a gypsy's.

Slowly his gray eyes took in the regulation black pants and gray shirt she wore, then shot her a cold, dispassionate glance. Not by a twitch of the tiny scar at the corner of his mouth did he let her know that her presence affected him.

"Gina. I'm not even going to try to guess why you've shown up here—let alone outfitted like that. I'm on duty for the next twenty-four hours. If this has something to do with alimony payments, call your attorney. He's still in the phone book. Presuming you plan to be in town that long."

He reached for his magazine again, but she noted with satisfaction that his gaze fell on the hurry-ups propped next to her shoes, and his dark brows furrowed in displeasure. She had his attention at last! The standard-issue black boots, pants, helmet and yellow coat stood ready beside her. As if in slow motion his stormy eyes played over her face and figure once more, fastening on her slender waist where she'd attached her walkie-talkie.

At this point he rose to his full six feet two inches, looking leaner and fitter than she'd ever seen him. In full dress uniform he was heartbreakingly handsome. "If this is some kind of joke, I'm not amused."

She cleared her throat. "You asked for a replacement while Whittaker is on a leave of absence. I'm swinging in from Engine House Number 3. Call Captain Carrera if you want."

He scowled. "Captain Carrera is a pushover for a pretty face. What's going on, Gina?" he asked in a wintry tone. "Where did you get that turnout gear?"

"In San Francisco, when I graduated and started to work." She pulled her badge out of her shirt pocket and put it on top of the magazine. He stared at the official insignia of the Salt Lake City Fire Department as if he'd never seen it before. His hand closed over the badge.

"Your approach is very novel, Gina, but enough's enough. I'm warning you—"

"Hey, Grady! I'm in!" One of the fire fighters poked his head inside the door, took one look at Gina and grinned. "Oops! Sorry, Captain. Just wanted you to know I'm here." Gina couldn't look at Grady as the fire fighter walked through the engine house calling, "Eighty-six! Eighty-six!" It was the code that meant a woman was on the premises. Everyone would be on his best behavior.

"Captain?" A man who seemed close to fifty knocked on the door and then came in without asking. "I'm going to fuel the truck unless you have other work assigned for me right now."

"Go ahead," Grady muttered.

"Ma'am." The older fire fighter nodded politely to Gina before leaving them alone once more. Following his exit four other men came into Grady's office on the pretext of checking in, but Gina was well aware of the real reason, and she had an idea that Grady was, too. Her gilt-blond hair drew attention wherever she went. In an effort to minimize her attractiveness, she wore it in a ponytail while on duty, but she had no way of hiding her unusual violet eyes with their dark lashes. As Grady had once told her, no other woman he'd ever met possessed her unique coloring—then he'd whispered that she was some kind of miracle as he pulled her into his arms. But she knew those memories had no place here today.

"All right, now that you've gained the attention of the entire department," he said, pointedly eyeing the last man out of the door before flicking her a hostile glance, "I'm afraid you'll have to leave."

Gina stood her ground but Grady would never know what it cost her to remain upright when her legs felt like buckling. "You requested a replacement because you're a person short. I'm the one who's been sent."

His eyes narrowed to silvery slits. "If you're a fire fighter, I'm Mary Poppins!"

Warmth suffused her cheeks. "Call headquarters. They'll verify my status as a paramedic, as well."

"I don't have time to listen to this," he bit out. "Goodbye, Gina. Whatever it is you want can be accomplished through the mail. I believe I've made myself clear. The door is be—"

"Ladder 1 respond to concession fire in Liberty Park area." The dispatcher's voice over the gong accomplished what nothing else could have. A fire fighter's sole function was to respond to the alarm once it sounded. Grady left her standing there as if she didn't exist and ran to the truck. Already she could hear the revving of the engine and shouts from the men. And she could feel the familiar surge of adrenaline that fills every fire fighter's veins once a call comes. It was as natural as breathing for her to want to respond, but she'd been assigned to engine 1. So therefore she had no choice but to go inside and settle in until the gong sounded for their rescue unit.

The truck left the station, its siren wailing, within twenty seconds of the time the alarm had come in. Anything under a minute was good, Gina mused, feeling inordinately proud of the work Grady did. So many times in their short-lived marriage, he'd tried to explain this pride and sense of exhilaration to her, but she hadn't understood. In all honesty, she hadn't wanted to. Out of fear that he might get killed, she'd accused him of trying to be a macho man who got his kicks from playing with fire.

How wrong she'd been. How little she'd understood what motivated him. Not until she'd been through the rigorous training herself had she begun to comprehend his love of fire fighting. It gave him a natural high that not even his work as a correspondent, covering explosive situations in the Middle East and Central America, had offered. That high was contagious and had finally infected her. But how to make *him* see that?

She reached down for her turnout gear, aware that seeing Grady for the first time since the divorce had shaken her badly. She'd rehearsed the moment a thousand times in her mind, imagining—fearing—it would go exactly as it did. But his indifference to her physical presence managed to twist the knife a little deeper, dissolving her hopes that somewhere inside him he still cared.

If he'd been told ahead of time that she worked for the fire department and was being sent to his station, he'd have been on the phone to the battalion chief to protest. She wouldn't have been able to get near him.

This way, she had the slight advantage of cornering him in his own territory. She knew enough about her ex-husband to realize he detested making his private business public. He wouldn't be able to get rid of her in front of the others without creating an embarrassing scene.

So when he came back and found her in residence, he'd have to live with the fact until they could be completely alone. A shiver crept along her spine at the thought of that confrontation, but too much was at stake for her to back down now.

As a friend had once innocently said when Gina admitted she was still in love with Grady, "Then stop moaning about it. Go after him! Fight fire with fire!" Gina had done exactly that. And she'd come face-to-face with a man whose eyes were as dead to her as the ashes of last winter's grate fire.

Someone's tuneless whistle broke in on her thoughts. One of the men she'd seen a few minutes ago came into the office on a lope, but he stopped short when he noticed her gear. His light blue eyes smiled. "Hi. I'm Lieutenant Corby. You must be Ron Whittaker's replacement."

"That's right. I'm Gina Lindsay." She shook his outstretched hand with difficulty because of the helmet and boots she carried, and they both laughed. The sandy-haired man didn't seem to take himself too seriously. Gina liked that.

"Since the captain's not here, I'll show you around. For a minute there, we all thought you were his latest conquest.'' Relieving her of the boots, he grinned in a mischievous manner that exuded confidence.

Gina fought to keep the smile pasted on her face. "The captain has a reputation, does he?" she asked as she followed him into the large room behind the office that served as a living room cum lounge.

"Only after hours. He's a stickler for the rules. Fortunately for me, I'm not. You married?"

"You're straightforward, I'll grant you that, Lieutenant, so I'll return the favor. I'm not married but I made an ironclad rule when I became a fire fighter— no mingling with the crew except on a professional basis.'' In fact, she hadn't accepted a date since her return to Salt Lake and generally preferred the company of Susan Orr, a fire fighter from engine 5.

"Not ever?" His mock expression of pain made her laugh again, and this in turn brought two other men out of the kitchen, carrying mugs of coffee.

"Howard? Ed? Meet Gina. She's the swing-in for Whittaker."

The men said hello and eyed her speculatively, but not with the same glimmer of male admiration they'd displayed earlier when they thought she was a visitor. She'd come to expect this reaction from her male co-workers. Only in recent years had women intruded on their all-male fraternity.

Gina tried hard to blend into the background and not call attention to herself. Most of the fire fighters she knew were becoming accustomed to females in the department, but a few still had trouble accepting women in the traditionally male role. She could understand their feelings. She was a woman, and that made a difference in their eyes. It always would. The only thing to do was try to get along, and for the most part Gina had succeeded. But it took time to ease in and become a part of the family.

"You can bunk in that bed next to the wall," the lieutenant continued, setting her boots down beside it. He gave her a quick tour of the kitchen, bathroom and dorm. "We've all eaten breakfast, but there's plenty left if you're hungry."

"Thanks. I might take you up on that after I settle in."

"Grab it while you can. We get busy around here. Working under the captain, you'll learn stuff that wasn't in the textbooks. Here. Let me put your coat and helmet out by the truck, and call me Bob when the captain's not around. Okay?"

"Okay." Once again, she relinquished her things to him without the argument that she could do it herself. Some men couldn't break the habit of treating her like a woman instead of simply a co-worker. She didn't mind at all.

Once alone, she surveyed her kingdom. Eight beds and eight individual lockers took up most of the dorm's space. She straightened her hurry-ups and threw her small overnight bag on the bed, pulling out a pair of coveralls before she went into the bathroom to dress. She expected to be uncomfortably warm; the weatherman predicted ninety-eight degrees by midafternoon, a typical July day. However, she liked the dry heat of Utah after the dampness of the Coast.

Gina forced herself to eat a light breakfast, but any second she expected to hear the truck returning to the station and the sound of Grady's deep voice issuing orders. She decided to do without coffee because she didn't need a stimulant. The dispatcher's voice coming periodically over the radio kept her adrenaline flowing at a fairly steady pace. That, combined with the fact that she'd be working with Grady, had her heart pumping overtime as it was.

"We're going to play tennis before it gets too hot," Bob called out from the next room. "You ready?"

"I'll be right there." She finished putting her dishes in the cupboard and ran out of the kitchen. Howard and Ed were already on board the engine. Bob held the door open for her, but to her dismay she could hear the ladder truck already entering the bay.

"Ms Lindsay. If I could have a word with you," Grady ordered as he jumped off the rig that had backed into the station. He tossed his helmet on the peg and walked over to her, his eyes a smoldering black. He was her superior, so Gina had no choice but to obey. She removed her booted foot from the step.

"Next time," Bob promised. The other men waved and the engine roared off.

Gina followed Grady to his office with trepidation, while the other men headed for the kitchen. She sensed Grady had now had time for the shock to wear off. Inside the office, he turned around and leaned against the door, arms folded. His silence, ominous and unforgiving, made her feel uneasy, and she sought refuge in one of the chairs facing his desk.

"I hoped you'd be gone when we came back, but I suppose it was too much to ask for. You've got exactly one minute to tell me what this is all about." She heard the underlying threat in his tone.

"I'm not the person you should be asking since I have no validity in your eyes," she answered calmly. "Call anybody at number 3. I've been working there for two months, and before that, in Carmel and San Francisco. Yesterday Captain Carrera told me my orders were to report here this morning."

A nasty smile pulled at the corner of his mouth. "Are you honestly trying to tell me that the woman I divorced because of irreconcilable differences to do with my job—among other things—is now a fully certified fire fighter?"

"Yes." Her chin lifted a fraction.

"Forgive me, but my imagination simply won't stretch that far."

Gina got to her feet, needing to choose her words carefully. "Grady, I don't blame you for being incredulous, but a lot has happened in the past three years."

A dark brow quirked disdainfully. "You're asking too much if you expect me to believe you've become an entirely different person in that period of time. The word *fire* used to scare the life out of you."

"That's true," she said forcefully, "until I sought professional help."

"That's an interesting revelation, considering the fact that you point-blank refused to get help all the time we were married." The cords stood out in his bronzed neck. "I begged you to talk to someone. I'd have done anything if I thought it would do any good, but you weren't interested."

"You're wrong, Grady. I was too *frightened*." She wiped her moist palms against her hips in an unconscious gesture of frustration and uncertainty. "Don't you see? If I couldn't be helped, then it would have been worse than ever! I was afraid of the answer."

His mouth thinned to a white line. "But *after* our divorce you suddenly found the courage. That pretty well says it all, doesn't it, Gina?"

"Engine 1 respond to medical assist at 1495 Washington Boulevard."

Grady unexpectedly reached out and grasped her wrist. "Let's find out what kind of fire fighter you've become...with paramedic training to boot! And when we get back you can further enlighten me as to why you've returned to the scene of the crime. I'm not through with you, Gina. Not by a long shot!"

He perforce had to let go of her arm as they entered the lounge. "Winn? You'll ride engine for now. I'm going on this assist." He rapped out the order as they hurried to the ladder truck. Gina could still feel the imprint of Grady's hand on her wrist by the time they arrived at their destination on the west side of town.

Grady rarely lost control in any situation, and the ferocity of his grip told her she'd hit a nerve, one that ran deep.

Rico drove the truck. Next to him sat Frank, then Gina. Grady got in last and shut the door. She was almost sick with excitement at being this close to him after all these years. His body remained rigid. No one in the department would ever have guessed how intimate she and their revered captain had once been. He showed no feelings for her now except a residue of bitterness that her presence had suddenly evoked.

Still, she was where she'd wanted desperately to be. There'd been times during the past few years when she wondered if she'd ever realize her dream of being with Grady again.

As they pulled up to a white frame bungalow Grady made the assignments. "Gina will be patient man, Rico, you stay with the rig. Frank, you and I will supply backup. Let's go."

Gina followed Grady off the truck and strode quickly to the front porch, where a middle-aged woman stood waiting just inside the screen door. She held up her left hand, and Gina could see that her ring finger was swollen twice its size, constricted by her wedding rings.

"Thank heavens you came," she blurted out, white with pain. "I didn't know what to do. Once in a while I break out in hives, but this sneaked up on me. I can't get my rings off and I'm afraid I'll lose my finger."

"We're here in plenty of time to prevent that from happening," Gina assured her. "Let's go into the kitchen. The table is a perfect place for you to lie down while we get those rings off. I'll just grab a pillow off your couch, and Frank will go out to the truck to get the cutter. What's your name?" As Gina conversed with the woman, Grady stood a few feet away scrutinizing her every move.

"Mary Fernandez." The woman sighed as she climbed up on the table with Gina's help and lay flat on her back.

"Well, Mary Fernandez," Gina said, smiling, "we'll have you comfortable within a half hour. What have you taken for the pain?"

"Aspirin."

"Good. That will help."

"Is it bad?" the woman asked anxiously.

"Swelling often seems worse than it really is. What I don't like to do is cut into your rings. They're beautiful."

"I think so," Mary said. "My husband's away on business. He won't believe this."

"Well, now you'll have something exciting to tell him," Gina soothed, taking the cutter from Frank. "It will hurt for a while because I have to get the underside of the saw around the band. I'm going to cut through in three places. If you want to scream, I won't mind."

"I had five children and never screamed." She chuckled, but Gina could see the way the woman was biting her lip.

As incident commander, Grady had to write a report, and he made notes, asking a few questions while Gina continued to saw carefully through the gold bands. Twenty minutes later, the swollen red finger was free of the constriction.

"Ah..." The woman moaned her relief, and her eyes filled with tears. "You're an angel from heaven and you look like one, too. Thank you."

"You're welcome." Gina assisted the woman to her feet and handed her the pieces of her wedding bands. "These can be made to look like new again."

The older woman smiled. "It doesn't matter. My finger's more important."

"Indeed it is. Do you know what causes your hives?"

"No, but I'm going to call a doctor and find out so nothing like this ever happens again."

"Well, you take care of yourself, Mary. Call us again if you're ever in trouble."

"I will," she murmured, walking them to the door. "What's your name? I want to write a letter to the department to let them know how grateful I am for what you did."

"Just call us station 1. Goodbye, Mary." Gina shook hands with the woman before going outside to the truck. By now a medium-sized crowd had gathered around. This time, Gina was last to climb onto the rig.

"How many times have you done that maneuver?" Frank wanted to know as they drove into the mainstream of traffic.

"That was my first."

"You could have fooled me. You have a real nice way about you, Gina. Welcome aboard."

"Thanks. Actually, the woman was wonderful. That had to hurt!"

"Rico, pull over at the next supermarket. We'll grab a bite of lunch." Grady's suggestion effectively changed the topic of conversation.

"Will do, Captain. Who wants to go in on barbecued spareribs?"

"I do." Gina and Frank both spoke at the same time. Under normal circumstances, Gina had a healthy appetite but was fortunate to have a metabolism that kept her nicely rounded figure on the slender side. When she worked a particularly busy and demanding shift, she ate what the men did. Fire fighting devoured calories.

"How about you, Captain?" Rico inquired.

"I don't know. I'll wait till I get in there."

Rico parked in an alley and they all went inside the store. They'd just made their purchases when another call came through on their walkie-talkies. By the time they reached the scene of a car that was on fire, it had burned itself out. Grady made a preliminary report, and then they headed back to the station, eating their food on the way.

Since the bathroom wasn't in use when they returned, Gina slipped inside to wash up, thinking she'd relax on her bunk for a while and read the latest issue of *Firework*. But when she walked into the dorm, her cot wasn't there. Puzzled, she went over to the locker, but all her belongings had disappeared.

"I took the liberty of moving your bed and gear to my office, in case you were wondering."

Gina whirled around. "Why would you do that?"

"Because there's no way you're sleeping with seven men," Grady said in an authoritative voice that brooked no argument. They were still alone in the dorm.

"I've never asked for special privileges and I don't intend to start now. It's bad for morale, and I don't want to be singled out."

"In this station, you do it my way, Gina."

"At number 3 the four of us slept in the same room."

His gray eyes glittered dangerously. "Perhaps now that you've left, they'll be able to get some sleep."

"There are five women in the department and—"

"Half of my crew is married." His face wore a shuttered expression. "I won't allow you to create any undue stress among the wives by sleeping in the same room with their husbands."

"Do you think I'd intentionally try to cause trouble?" Her chest heaved with indignation.

"It follows you, Gina."

"When we were married I don't recall making a fuss because you slept in the same room with female fire fighters."

His mouth twisted in a mockery of a smile. "You have a short memory. When we were married, there were no women in the department. It made life a whole lot easier."

His tone made her wonder if he was one of those men who didn't approve of female fire fighters on principle, but this was not the time to get into that particular discussion. "The crew will know something's wrong."

He paused on his way out the door. "Don't lose any sleep over it. By your next shift, you'll be back at engine 3," he stated with familiar arrogance.

"You can't do that, Grady!" she retorted without thinking. She'd only been on duty seven hours and already he wanted her as far away from him as possible.

"Can't I!" He fixed her with a glacial stare. "Just watch me!"

"I didn't mean it that way." She took a deep breath. "I understand Whittaker will be out several more weeks."

"How typical of you, Gina. Now you're certified, you think you're the only paramedic in the department."

She bit her lip in an effort not to rise to the bait. "I don't want to be switched back before the allotted time because it won't look good on my record," she lied. Under no circumstances could she tell Grady the real reason.

"Don't worry." He grimaced and looked at his watch. "Seventeen more hours—after that you're home free. Captain Carrera will understand when I tell him I've found someone else with more years in the department to fill in."

"So you won't give me a chance!" She fought to keep her voice steady.

A nerve twitched alongside his strong jaw. "I'm giving you the same chance you gave *us*, Gina. And now you have approximately five minutes before you're to report to the lounge. We're going to discuss a variety of prefire plans, and we'd all be fascinated by a contribution from you."

Her delicate brows furrowed. "What do you mean?"

"You trained in San Francisco. Maybe there's something you can teach us," he muttered sarcastically.

"Grady..." Her eyes pleaded for a little understanding.

"Captain Simpson to you, *Ms Lindsay*." He passed a couple of the men on his way out of the dorm. Gina could hear their voices pitched low, then suddenly something Grady said made them burst out laughing. It shouldn't have hurt, but it did....

CHAPTER TWO

WITH ONLY A FEW MINUTES to go until the next shift reported for duty, Gina got up and dressed, made her bed and slipped out the front door of the station carrying her turnout gear.

She hurried to the private parking lot out back and put her things in the Honda, not wanting to be cornered by Grady. Her first twenty-four hours at station 1 had been enlightening. Fortunately, both the engine and the ladder were kept busy throughout the night, preventing Grady from catching her alone. From time to time, she'd sensed his gaze on her, eyes narrowed in anger, but she didn't acknowledge him unless directly addressed.

A car passed her in the driveway as she pulled out into the street. She expelled a sigh, relieved that she'd managed to escape him, but she knew it was only a temporary respite. Still, she couldn't face him right now. Too many emotions and memories were tearing her apart. She needed a little distance to regain her perspective before he forced a confrontation—and knowing Grady, there would be one....

Traffic was fairly heavy with people anxious to get to work. While she waited through the third red light at the same intersection, she happened to glance in the rearview mirror. The black Audi several cars behind her wasn't familiar, but she recognized the man at the wheel. Her heart did a funny kick. Was it coincidence or was Grady following her?

Three quarters of the way home to her apartment on the East bench, he still pursued her. Evidently he wanted to get their talk out of the way as soon as possible. A thrill of fear darted through her. His anger had been growing since she reported for duty the morning before. Right now she imagined that one wrong word from her might rip away that civilized veneer to reveal the bitter, uncompromising man who'd divorced her.

When she drove into the carport of the duplex she rented, Grady was out of his car and opening her door before she could pull the key from the ignition. "You still drive too fast, Gina."

"Apparently not fast enough," she muttered, sliding out of the driver's seat.

"Something told me I wouldn't find you at home if I came by later." He accompanied her to the front door and stood there, patiently waiting for her to unlock it. She was dismayed to find that her hand trembled. This was *Grady* about to enter her house. She'd imagined it so many times—but not when they'd both just come off duty, dead tired and still wearing their uniforms. Now was not the time for the kind of talk Grady had in mind.

"Come in." She finally found her voice, wondering too late what he would think about her gallery of photographs, covering two entire walls. Many of the pictures were of him, some taken on their honeymoon in Egypt, others in Carmel during a visit to her parents. But he walked into her small living room without looking around him, his attention focused solely on her. He gave nothing away. His study of her face was almost clinical.

Unable to help herself, Gina stared at him. The first thing she noticed was that he needed a shave. His beard was as black as his curly hair. It gave him a slightly dissipated air that added to his masculine appeal. Without her intending them to, her eyes roamed over the familiar lines and angles of his features and settled on his mouth, a mouth that could curve with a sensuality so beguiling she'd forget everything else.

Three years hadn't changed him, not really. It was more in the way he responded to the people around him that be betrayed a new hardness and cynicism. But maybe it was just with her that he exhibited this dark side. She wondered if the laughing, loving Grady she adored had gone for good—and worse, if she'd been the person to rob him of that joie de vivre.

The tempestuous battles leading up to their divorce had killed all the love he'd felt for her. In three years he hadn't once tried to contact her by phone or letter. Like flash fire, their love had burned hot, out of control, sweeping them along in a euphoric blaze. Then suddenly it blew itself out, and she wakened to a nightmare.

"Would you like something to eat or drink?"

"Gina—" he bit out, quickly losing patience with her as he lodged against the arm of the couch. She sat down on the matching sofa across from him. His eyes were a startling gray, impaling her like lasers. "What's going on? What are you doing back in Salt Lake? I'd like an honest answer."

Gina settled back against the cushions and crossed her legs, trying to assume a nonchalance she didn't feel. He wanted honesty but she didn't dare give him that. Not once in twenty-four hours had he shown the least sign that he still had any feelings for her.

All this time she'd held the hope that seeing her again would trigger some kind of positive reaction, however small, however ambivalent.

"I used to live here, Grady."

"More to the point, you died here," he came back in a harsh tone of voice. "The person you were, the marriage we had . . . all dead."

She swallowed hard. "It felt that way at the time—until I sought counseling and started examining the reasons for my so-called phobia."

"Which were?"

"We married without really knowing anything about each other. There I was, teaching English in Beirut, then suddenly I met you and within six weeks we were husband and wife. Our married life in the Middle East was like one long, extended honeymoon with no home base and—"

"And dangerous," he inserted icily. "Certainly as life-threatening as any work I do now, but I don't recall your giving it a thought. If I remember correctly, you were more than eager to be my bride."

Gina averted her eyes. "Grady—" her voice trembled "—you told me that the newspaper you worked for had offered you an editor's job and that you intended to take it so we could start a family. I thought that was why we made our home in Salt Lake. You told me you craved a little domesticity. But after sitting at that desk for a few weeks, you dropped a bomb on me. Without discussing any of it, you resigned and told me you were going to go back to your old job of fire fighting." She got to her feet and began pacing. "I didn't even know you'd been a fire fighter. I thought you'd always been a newspaperman."

"I believe we covered this ground three years ago, Gina."

"And I'm trying to explain to you that I was too young and immature at the time to understand your needs. You were right when you accused me of being spoiled, incapable of giving support or comfort to my husband. It wasn't just my fears of your job. I've never told you this before but I was jealous of your friendship with the crew. I felt like you loved the fire fighters more than you loved me."

Something flickered in the recesses of his eyes, but he let her go on talking. For the first time she felt that maybe he was listening.

"Don't you see? I wanted to fulfill you in every way, but when you started fire fighting again, I thought you must have fallen out of love with me, that I no longer brought you the kind of happiness you needed. As a result, I felt totally inadequate. The psychologist explained that I used the fear of fire to mask my *real* fear of losing you. Perhaps that doesn't make sense to you, but it opened my eyes."

"Go on."

She took a deep breath. "Further along in therapy, I was challenged to explore my fear of fire. The psychologist suggested I observe a fire fighter training session. You see, long after we divorced I was plagued by nightmares, all having to do with fire."

He rubbed the back of his bronzed neck as she spoke. The fact that he didn't interrupt told her he was absorbed in what she had to say.

"Well, I went to a few training sessions and watched and learned. Incredibly, my nightmares went away and I actually found myself wanting to be a participant. The psychologist was right after all. I didn't have a fear of fire. Eventually, one of the trainers suggested I take the examination to see if I could qualify for the school. This didn't happen overnight, of course, but in time I took it and passed, and went on from there."

Grady stared at her for timeless minutes without saying anything. She couldn't imagine what he was thinking.

"Do you remember telling me what it was like to fight and the indescribable feeling you got from helping people?" Her violet eyes beseeched his understanding. "I couldn't relate to that at all. It just made me feel more isolated from you than ever, but—"

"But another miracle occurred and now you understand me completely," he mocked.

"Not completely," she answered, struggling to keep her voice calm, "but I can honestly say I share your love of fire fighting."

His face closed up. "So why didn't you stay in California?"

If only she dared tell Grady what was in her heart, but the very remoteness of his expression prevented her from blurting out her love for him. "I—I suppose deep down I wanted to show you that I had overcome my fear. I knew you'd never believe me unless you actually saw me on the job."

"You're right about that," he said thickly.

"Grady," she began, her voice almost a whisper, "I discovered something else in my counseling sessions. You and I parted with a great deal of bitterness, for which I take most of the blame." She watched his dark brows draw together. "I hoped that if I came back to Salt Lake we could meet as friends and bury past hurts."

He got to his feet, holding himself rigid. "That's asking the impossible, Gina."

She bit her lip and nodded. "Then I'll just have to accept that. I realize our marriage failed mostly because of me. I had this idea that if you heard me say it, it might help to heal some of the wounds. Despite everything, I've always wanted your happiness. And I've always hoped you didn't blame yourself for problems that weren't your fault. You're a fire fighter's fire fighter. I was a naive little fool to expect you to quit and find something safe and sane to do for the rest of your life. Perhaps a part of me wants your forgiveness.''

His eyes were shuttered. ''Forgiveness doesn't come into it, Gina. I was insensitive to your fears and needs, too.'' She had the impression he was about to say something else and then changed his mind. ''I'm glad you got the counseling you needed, but I'm sorry you made the move to Salt Lake to prove something that wasn't necessary. I followed you here because I was afraid you'd come to Utah with the mistaken notion that we could pick up where we left off three years ago.''

She felt like dying. ''No. We're both different people now. Firehouse gossip says you have interests elsewhere.''

Grady's intent gaze swept over her. ''You've grown up, Gina, and it's all to the good. But it doesn't change the way I feel about your working at station 1.''

She thrust out her chin. ''I figured that was why you followed me home. Well, where do I report for duty tomorrow, or should I call headquarters?''

He didn't say anything for a minute. In the past she'd fought him on everything. Right now he was probably in shock that she was being so amenable. ''There will be talk if I switch you to another station before Whittaker comes back, particularly as there were no complaints about your performance. Far be it from me to give you a black mark on your record after one shift because of personal considerations. You can stay on, Gina, until Whittaker reports back, which should be two weeks at the most. But in the meantime, I suggest you bid another couple of stations if you intend to live in Salt Lake.''

Two weeks at the most to accomplish the impossible! ''I'll take your advice. Thank you, Grady,'' she whispered, suppressing her joy that he hadn't seen fit to send her out of his domain just yet.

For some reason, Grady didn't seem to like this new side of her, or at least, he didn't seem to know how to respond to her levelheaded behavior. ''When you report in the morning, you'll be treated exactly like everyone else.''

''Of course.''

''Stay away from Frank. He already thinks he's in love with you. He's got a sweet wife at home.''

She blinked. ''Anything else?''

''Corby's been telling everybody that you don't date fire fighters, but he's going to be the first one to make you break your rule. Don't do it, Gina. It can ruin lives.''

They stared at each other across the expanse. ''I never have and I never will. Is that good enough for you?''

''You're the one I'm worried about. To be a professional means never to mix business with pleasure. To be a woman in this profession makes it that much more difficult.''

Gina smiled. ''Do I take it you don't approve of female fire fighters?''

He started walking toward the front door. ''Did I say that?'' he shot back.

"I'm not sure. I don't remember you expressing your opinion one way or the other when we were married."

"The issue never came up." He gave her an enigmatic look.

"Now that it has, would you tell me your honest feelings?" She'd heard every opinion under the sun, but Grady's was the only one that mattered to her.

He appeared to consider her question for a minute. "If a woman can do her job well, it makes no difference to me."

"But—" Gina added, sensing a certain hesitancy on his part.

He rubbed the back of his neck thoughtfully. "But I still prefer to retain the image of a woman as I see her. Soft, curvaceous, warm, sweet-smelling...

"I'm afraid a woman in turnout gear with a mask and Nomex hood loses something in the translation. Particularly when her ears are singed, her knees burned beyond recognition and her face blackened with third-degree burns that never heal properly."

Gina was inordinately pleased with his answer. She cocked her head to the side. "It's a cosmetic thing with you, then."

"I suppose. However, you proved today that you could do the job. So admirably, in fact, that both crews want to hear more from you the next time we discuss prefire procedures. Your comment about always wearing your mask to the scene of a car fire made an impact. In the crew's words, you're all right. High praise indeed after only one shift. Does that answer your question?" He sounded bored with the whole discussion.

"Yes, but I have one more. Have you told anyone—does anyone know about—"

"About us?" he interjected sternly. "No, Gina, and I see no reason for it to ever become public knowledge."

She lowered her eyes. "No. Of course not." Her bottom lip quivered and she bit it. "What shall I call you at the station? Captain or Grady? The men call you both, depending on circumstances."

He reached for the front doorknob. "Do whatever moves you, Gina."

She drew closer, smiling inside. She wondered what he'd do if she ever called him "darling" or "sweetheart," the way she used to. Neither of them would be able to live it down in front of the crew, but right now she was tempted. "Well, I'll see you in the morning."

Grady's pewter eyes played over her features once more before he nodded. Then he was out the door.

She started to shut it but left it open a crack so she could watch him as he strode quickly toward his car and drove away. She hungered for the sight of him and wondered how she would make it through the next twenty hours until she could be with him again.

He'd never know how close she'd come to walking over and putting her arms around him. No matter what their problems, they'd never had trouble communicating physically. As soon as they were within touching distance, the cares of the world would vanish. Grady was a passionate lover, always tender and seemingly insatiable. She'd never been intimate with a man until Grady came into her life. After three years, she still couldn't imagine being with anyone else. He'd ruined her for other men; if it was too late for her and Grady now, she had the strong conviction she'd remain single for the rest of her life.

Tears spilled down her cheeks. She missed him terribly. He was the most wonderful thing ever to come into her life, but she'd been too insecure to handle the fact that he lived another life apart from her—a dangerous one.

That was why, at thirty-three, he had an enviable collection of medals for heroism, according to Captain Carrera, and a reputation throughout the city that few men could equal.

Only the most aggressive fire fighters would bid for the kind of action he and others like him faced every time they reported for duty. That reality had paralyzed Gina with fear throughout their marriage. Now she quietly preened at all the praise heaped on her ex-husband.

If she didn't have to keep her former relationship with Grady a secret, she could entertain the guys with several hair-raising accounts of his daring in Beirut and Nicaragua during his war correspondent days. They'd never hear about it otherwise, because Grady was so modest—always had been. He couldn't see that what he did was in any way out of the ordinary.

To Gina, her husband had been bigger than life. But she'd loved Grady with a possessive love and lost him. If he'd only give them another chance, she longed to show him how different their marriage could be. There had to be a way to reach him, and she'd find it no matter how long that took!

Naturally Grady would have been with other women since their divorce, but so far no other woman had captivated him to the point that he'd proposed marriage. As far as Gina was concerned, her ex-husband was fair game and she would break any rule to win him back. With luck, Whittaker wouldn't return as quickly as Grady envisioned, giving her more time to rekindle his interest. Then maybe he'd learn to like the woman she'd become—enough to want to see her off duty.

Happier than she'd been in three years, Gina cleaned her apartment from top to bottom, showered, then took a long nap. Later in the day she went to dinner and a movie with her friend, Sue.

They'd met when a fellow fire fighter was injured and taken to the burn unit at University Hospital. During their all-night vigil they hit it off famously. When they had free days at the same time, they often watched videos and ordered pizza. Susan was down on policemen at the moment, having dated one who turned out to be married.

She and Susan had quite a lot in common, personally and professionally, and it amazed Gina now to think that during the months she lived in Salt Lake with Grady, she'd never once gone down to the station house or met any of his crew. She hadn't made any new friends, particularly avoiding people connected with Grady's line of work. Her life had been far too insular, always waiting for Grady to come home.

She hadn't wanted anyone else if she couldn't have him. He must have felt so trapped, she mused sadly.

When Gina reported for work the next morning, she could hardly contain her excitement, because she and Grady would be spending the next twenty-four hours under the same roof. Her eyes searched for him hungrily as she let herself in the front door of the station, dressed in coveralls. He and the others had already started their routine jobs of checking out the apparatus. Everything had to work, from the siren to the lights. All the breathing equipment had to be in perfect condition.

"Good morning," she called out. The men turned in her direction to greet her. She was conscious of their staring, but it was Grady's gray eyes she sought. To make sure he never forgot that she was a warm, sweet-smelling, curvaceous woman, she'd left her hair long and brushed it until it gleamed a silvery gold. Behind her ears she'd applied a new, expensive perfume Grady wouldn't recognize, but she wore little makeup except lipstick. She returned everyone's smiles, noting that Grady was the only one who merely glanced at her and nodded while he continued to inspect the pump gauges.

"What's my assignment for this morning, Captain?"

"You can start with the windows in the station."

"All right." She headed for the kitchen to fill a pan with hot water and vinegar. No fire fighter loved doing the station's housekeeping duties, but washing windows was definitely the most abhorrent and demeaning assignment of all. Bathrooms rated higher.

Gina settled down to her task with a vengeance. Grady knew exactly what he was doing—and he wasn't playing fair. He said he'd treat her like the others, but that obviously wasn't the case. There were enough windows in the place to keep her busy and isolated all day, which was exactly his intention. He purposely didn't assign any of the men to help with the job because he didn't want her fraternizing with one individual. She knew Grady was determined to keep her as far away from him as possible, without letting the crew suspect his intentions. And his word was law.

When the gong sounded for engine 1 to respond to a medical assist because of a family fight, Gina had to leave her window washing unfinished and hurry out to the truck. Grady had warned them that the Fourth of July holiday would bring a lot of calls. Unfortunately Grady rode ladder, which meant she'd see him only in passing. But even in that assumption she was wrong. After they'd assisted at the stabbing, their engine went immediately to a vacant lot where some children had started a fire while trying to light their "snakes."

The few times the engine returned to the station, the ladder truck was out. By eight that evening, the engine had responded to over twenty calls. Gina grabbed a bite to eat and quickly put the window-washing equipment away before another call came through. She'd have to finish the job on her next shift.

Around eleven, they were called to a house fire on the lower avenues. Grady's ladder was already in position when they pulled up to the scene. Gina gathered from Bob's conversation with the batallion chief over the walkie-talkie that the roof had caught fire from an illegal bottle rocket.

The sounds of fireworks and cherry bombs, the popping of firecrackers and the shrill whistling of noisemakers filled the hot night air. Everyone in Salt Lake seemed to be outside, which made driving to the scene much more difficult and gave Howard nightmares that he might run over someone's child suddenly darting into the street.

Smoke was pouring out the upstairs window and attic area of the huge old house. The enormous pine trees surrounding it could easily catch fire, something they all feared. Grady was up on the roof with the chain saw to ventilate. She could see his tall body silhouetted against the orange-red glow of the flames. The fire was becoming fully involved, which meant that every part of the structure was burning. Grady and his backup man would have to relinquish their position soon.

Gina was nozzle-handler and Ed, leadoff man. She entered the house with the empty hose; it was easier to manipulate without any water in it. She dashed up the old staircase to the second floor, then sent Ed back to tell the pump man to turn on the water. Another engine had been called to assist, and several hoses were going at once. It didn't take long to contain the fire.

Outside, while they were putting the hoses away a little while later, Gina glanced at the ladder truck but couldn't see Grady. She excused herself for a minute and hurried over to Frank. "Where's the captain?"

His perpetual grin was missing. "They hauled him to Holy Cross Hospital."

It felt as though a giant hand had squeezed her insides. "What happened?"

"I don't know. I was at the other end of the roof when it collapsed."

That was all Gina needed to hear. *Dear God,* she murmured to herself as she hurried back to the engine. "Howard, the captain's been injured."

"Yeah, I heard," he said when they'd all climbed inside. "We'll go by the hospital on the way back to the station and check up on him." No one spoke as they drove away from the scene. The bond between fire fighters was as strong as any blood ties could ever be, and she knew how the crew members felt about Grady.

All Gina could think about was that at least he hadn't been trapped inside the attic or wasn't still missing. Grady had often reminded them that no two fires were alike. The element of surprise lurking at every crisis made their work challenging and often dangerous. Gina tried to mask her feelings and let the others lead as they entered the emergency room.

To her surprise and everlasting gratitude, Grady was sitting on the end of the hospital bed being treated for smoke inhalation. As far as she could see nothing else was wrong.

The sight of four grubby, foul-smelling fire fighters drew everyone's attention, including Grady's. "Get out of here, you guys." He sounded strong and completely like himself. Gina sent up a silent prayer.

"We're going." Bob grinned and punched him in the shoulder. One way or another, all the men managed to give a physical manifestation of their affection and relief by a nudge or some other gesture. Gina kept her distance.

"I'll ride ladder if you'll finish washing my windows when we get back to the station." She spoke boldly with a smile that lit up her violet eyes. "I'd rather be treated for what you've got than these dishpan hands."

The guys hooted and hollered with laughter. Grady's steady gaze met hers. "No thanks. I'm on to a good thing and I know it. Those windows haven't been that squeaky clean since the place was built." A half smile lifted the corner of his mouth and her heart turned over. It was the first genuine, spontaneous smile he'd given her. If only he knew how she'd been waiting for that much of a response. Even if it had taken this crisis to make him forget for a little while the enmity between them, she was thankful. "I'll see you guys later," he muttered.

"Your captain won't be coming to work for at least forty-eight hours," the attending physician broke in. "It's home and total bed rest." Grady grimaced as the oxygen mask was put over his face again, but Gina rejoiced that the doctor had taken charge.

The ride to the station was entirely different from the earlier journey to the hospital. The men jabbered back and forth, releasing the nervous tension that had gripped them when they thought something might be seriously wrong with Grady. Gina felt positively euphoric and suggested they drop by the Pagoda for Chinese take-out—an idea applauded by everyone.

The station house was quiet after their last run. The men took their turns in the shower and when they'd finished, Gina took hers. Her thoughts ran constantly to Grady. He'd need some nursing when he got back to his condo. Was there a woman in his life, someone close enough to be there when he really needed help?

That question went around in her head all night. The hours dragged on endlessly. Except for one interruption—a call to put out a brush fire in the foothills—she should have had a good sleep by the time the shift ended at eight o'clock. Nothing could have been further from the truth. And judging from the looks on the faces of the crew, they, too, were concerned about Grady. When a couple of them said they were going to run by the captain's place before going home, she volunteered to go with them, adding that she knew a wonderful hot toddy recipe that soothed sore throats. They grinned at the idea of sampling her brew themselves, and as it turned out, all eight of them decided to visit their revered captain en masse. Gina could have hugged them. This way, she could see for herself that Grady was being looked after, and he couldn't possibly object to her presence—at least, not outwardly.

CHAPTER THREE

GRADY STILL LIVED in the condo Gina had shared with him during their brief marriage. Situated on a steep hill on the avenues high above Lindsay Gardens, its four floors of wood and glass looked out over the Salt Lake Valley in every direction. The stupendous view still had the power to take Gina's breath instantly, reviving a host of memories too painful to examine.

Winn did the phoning to gain them access, and one by one they filed up two flights of the spiral staircases to the third level, which Grady used as a living room cum lounge. Everything looked so exactly the same, Gina could scarcely believe it was three years since she'd stepped into this room with its café au lait and dark chocolate-brown accents. The fabulous Armenian rug they'd picked up on their travels still graced the parquet floor.

Standing in the corridor, she could see Grady lying on the brown leather couch in his familiar striped robe—one she'd worn as often as he after a passion-filled night of lovemaking. From this vantage point she couldn't tell his condition, but at least he was talking to the men. Needing to help, she went into the kitchen to make the drink of hot tea with touches of sugar, lemon and rum. She'd stopped at a store for the ingredients on the way, but had to rely on Grady's stock of spirits for the rum. Fortunately he had a quarter of a bottle on the shelf. She used it liberally then put it back, hoping no one would walk in on her in the process. The crew would become suspicious, to say the least, if they saw their newest rookie making herself at home in a strange kitchen, acting as if she belonged there.

She rummaged in the cupboard for a large mug. It didn't surprise her that the kitchen was immaculate. Grady had always kept a cleaner house than most women, with everything neatly in its place. She found a blue mug and poured the steaming liquid into it before hurrying upstairs, passing some of the crew on the way.

"I made enough for all of you," she called over her shoulder and walked toward Grady, now sitting up, propped against the cushions. The pupils of his eyes dilated in surprise at her approach. Apparently he hadn't known she'd come in with the others. She handed him the mug, taking care not to brush his fingers. "Try this, Captain. It's a proved remedy for what ails you."

He stared at her over the rim of the mug before taking a sip. "On whose authority?" At this point some of the others came up from the kitchen with drinks in their hands, ready to propose a toast to the captain's health.

"Mine. A couple of us were treated for smoke inhalation a few months ago. My buddy made this for me, and it really helped."

"It's not half-bad." Frank gave his seal of approval. The others took tentative tastes and echoed his opinion, then began drinking enthusiastically. Gina wondered if she was the only one who noticed the stillness that came over Grady after her explanation. He lifted the mug to his lips, but his unsmiling eyes didn't leave her face, almost as if the unexpected news had suddenly made him realize the dangers she'd been exposing herself to all this time. Was it her imagination, or did she detect a brief flash of anxiety in those gray eyes?

"You're not having any?" he asked after draining his mug. Everyone else was laughing and joking around, seemingly unaware of the tension between them.

Her mouth curved upward. "This stuff is potent. I have to be able to drive home."

"That's no problem. I'll see you get home safely," Bob piped up, bringing a roar of laughter from the crew.

"Don't you believe it," Howard whispered in her ear conspiratorially.

"Come on, guys," Bob bellowed. "Give me a break, will ya?"

Grady's mouth was pinched to a pencil-thin line, and Gina couldn't tell if it was the conversation or discomfort caused by his condition that produced the reaction. Either way, Gina didn't want their visit to add to his stress, and she began gathering mugs, including Grady's, to take back to the kitchen.

"Want some help?" Bob asked to the accompaniment of more laughter. He didn't know when to quit, she thought in annoyance.

She shook her head. "Don't you think one set of dishpan hands is enough, Lieutenant? You wouldn't want to ruin that macho image at this stage, would you?" This provoked more laughter, allowing her to escape Grady's unswerving stare and Bob's sudden frown.

She cleaned up the kitchen after preparing Grady a breakfast of eggs and toast. When Ed made an appearance with his mug she asked him to take Grady the plate of food. "Make sure he eats it, Ed. I've got to get going."

"Sure," he said, obviously surprised that she was leaving. But he didn't say anything else as she hurried from the kitchen and down the stairs to the front door.

A wall of heat enveloped her the moment she left Grady's air-conditioned condo to walk to her car. Salt Lake was experiencing an intense heat wave with no signs of letting up. Swimming in the pool at Susan's apartment building seemed an appealing prospect as Gina got into her car and drove home. This was her long weekend off, and already she could tell that she'd better fill it with activities or she'd go crazy thinking about Grady all alone in the condo. Or worse, with one of his girlfriends dropping by to keep him company. The pictures that filled her mind made her forget what she was doing, and it took a siren directly behind her to bring her back to awareness.

She glanced in her rearview mirror to see a police car signaling her to pull over. With a groan, she moved to the side of the boulevard above the cemetery and waited. A female officer approached the car and greeted Gina with a wry smile. Then the officer issued her a speeding ticket, her first since returning to Salt Lake. When she was free to go, she headed for Susan's apartment. They could both complain about the police—anything to take her mind off Grady.

As it turned out, Gina didn't get back to her own apartment until late that night, when she fell into a deep sleep almost before her head touched the pillow. She slept around the clock and awakened late in the morning to the sound of her mother's voice. The answering machine was still on. A twinge of guilt soon had Gina dialing her mother's number in Carmel. She hadn't written or phoned in more than three weeks, and she knew her mother worried.

They had a fairly long chat but by tacit agreement didn't discuss Grady. Her mother didn't approve of Gina's plan to insinuate herself into his life again. She'd argued from the beginning that Grady had married her under false pretenses, and as far as she was concerned, their marriage had been doomed at the outset because he hadn't revealed his love for fire fighting to Gina. Gina's father kept quiet on the subject, but she knew his opinion was the same as her mother's. They both hated her work.

The conversation ended after they made tentative plans for Gina to fly to California for the Labor Day weekend—one of the few holidays she didn't have to work.

. Before she took a shower, Gina played back the tape to see if she had any other messages. It annoyed her to hear Bob Corby's voice asking her to go out with him. He'd left his home number so she could call him back with her answer.

She felt the best thing to do was ignore the message, and the next time he approached her in person, reiterate her rules. In time, he had to get the point! She'd told Grady she didn't date the men she worked with, and she meant it. What Grady didn't know was that no man she'd ever met measured up to *him*—so there was no temptation, not even with the undeniably attractive Lieutenant Corby.

It took all Gina's self control not to call Grady or go by the condo to see if he was all right. When her next shift began, she arrived fifteen minutes early, only to discover that Grady wouldn't be in for a while. He had to be seen by a doctor before he could report for duty. Her spirits plummeted as she began housekeeping duties along with the others. She purposely avoided Bob, who followed her with his eyes. He was fast becoming a nuisance, but it wasn't until the gong sounded that she realized how angry he felt with her for not returning his call or even acknowledging it.

"Frank?" he shot out, issuing orders as the second in command. "Ms Lindsay will replace you on ladder this run."

Gina didn't know who was more surprised, she or Frank. The poor man looked as if Bob had just slapped him in the face. Clearly he wasn't happy about the sudden switch of assignment, but Gina understood. Bob had decided to set her up for failure. His ego couldn't stand being dented.

Handling ladders was difficult work, even for someone of Frank's brawn. Bob wanted her to look inadequate, unequal to the job.

Rico drove them out of the truck bay to the downtown area. It was noon, the worst possible time of day, with the heavy traffic impeding their progress. Bob got on his walkie-talkie with the battalion chief. They were discussing methods to proceed when Gina spotted smoke pouring out of a fourth-story window of the Duncan office building.

Engine 2 was first in, but the alarm had sounded for more help. This was it for Gina. If she made a mistake at the fire ground now, the other men would know it and possibly suffer as a result. She'd never be assigned to Ladder Number 1 again, and Grady would make sure she was relocated to the station that made the lowest number of runs. News of her failure would spread throughout the department. And this was exactly what Bob wanted to happen.

"Gina, you'll work with Winn, Rico with me. Let's go!"

Whether he'd set her up or not, right then Gina had a fire to fight. For the time being she forgot their personal battle and ran to the back of the truck. "I'll get the poles," she called out to Winn, who nodded and started pulling the ladder off the truck.

The trick with this kind of ladder was to attach the poles to the ladder on the ground and through leverage, hoist the ladder against the building. More than one person was needed to accomplish the maneuver. Gina had done it in training more times than she wanted to think about, but she'd hardly ever had to put it into practice during a real call.

Out of the corner of her eye she saw another ladder pull up to the fire ground. Already a couple of men from the engine truck had gone into the building with the hoses.

"Ready?" Winn shouted. Gina gave the sign and together they placed the ladder in an alley that gave access to the building and set it against the wall. Next she worked the rope that raised the extension so they could reach the fourth floor. She couldn't believe it but they managed the whole procedure without problems. Winn flashed her a quick smile that showed his relief. Normally it would have been Frank helping with the equipment, and she knew Winn had been holding his breath.

Gina grabbed her pack, then put the mask over her face before starting up the ladder. Her job was to hunt for any unconscious or injured people trapped in the building. She had no idea how involved the fire had become, but smoke continued to pour out of the fourth-floor windows and the atmosphere grew darker the higher she climbed.

Her turnout gear felt like a lead weight as she approached the top of the ladder to climb in one of the window frames, the glass blown out by the fire. She could only hope most of the people had left their offices to go to lunch before the outbreak.

The number 2 ladder truck working farther down the alley was having a tough time opening up the side of the building to ventilate. The smoke was really heavy now. Gina's intuition told her the hoses had probably extinguished most of the fire and what she was seeing was a lot of smoke from burned electrical insulation.

Finally she reached the window and wriggled in on her stomach. She started crawling around, going into one room and then another. It seemed like an eternity that she and Winn, who wasn't far behind, had been going around in circles. Except for the shout of a fire fighter and the sound of the hoses, she thought everyone else must have cleared the building. It was then she heard a low moan. The adrenaline surged through her.

Gina veered left and her gloved hand suddenly felt a body huddled up against the remains of a file cabinet. With the smoke as thick as mud Gina had no way of knowing if it was a woman or a man. But the body was definitely too heavy to lift.

Squatting, she grabbed the body under the arms and began to drag it, convinced the person was taller than her own five foot six.

The ventilation must have started working, because the smoke was now being drawn away from her. Gina inched along in the opposite direction, pulling the deadweight slowly down a watery, debris-filled corridor. She'd performed this maneuver hundreds of times in practice drills, but this was only her third live rescue. The instructors had told the class that there was no way to simulate the real thing, because practice drills didn't drain you emotionally and psychologically in quite the same way. They knew what they were talking about.

She encountered a nozzle-handler when she rounded a corner leading to a stairwell. Somewhere along the way she and Winn had become separated, so she was thankful when the man signaled to someone farther down the stairs on the hose to come and assist. The smoke had cleared sufficiently for her to see that she'd been dragging a man almost as big as Frank and completely unconscious. She and the other fire fighter managed to get the man down three flights of stairs and outside to the street.

Gina immediately pulled off her mask and put it on him. She flipped it on bypass to give the man air. He eventually started to come to as an ambulance crew took over and carted him away to a hospital. Clutching the mask she made her way back to the truck looking for Winn, but Rico said he hadn't come out yet.

With a sick feeling in the pit of her stomach, Gina hurried into the building again and raced up the stairs as fast as her turnout boots would allow. Dodging hoses, she replaced her mask and hurried along the floating wreckage, calling out for Winn. They worked on the buddy system. She wouldn't leave the building until she found him!

Panicking because she didn't get a response when she shouted, Gina moved quickly to the area where she'd entered through the window. A dozen different things could have gone wrong, and Winn could be anywhere, hurt or unconscious. She turned one corner on a run and careered into another fire fighter, the collision almost knocking the wind out of her. Her mask fell off. "Winn?" she cried out as the man holding her steady whisked off his own mask. "Grady!"

There was an indescribable look on his blackened face. She must have imagined he said, "Thank God," in a reverent whisper, because in the next instant he was giving her an order. "Go out to the truck, Gina."

"But I have to find Winn!"

"He's out on the ladder lifting someone to the ground right now. Do as I say!"

"But—"

"Don't argue with me," he thundered. "You've caused enough trouble already. Winn said you were up that ladder before he could stop you. You little fool. It wasn't intended that you enter the building on this run."

"But Lieutenant Corby—"

He muttered an epithet beneath his breath, and his hands tightened on her arms before releasing them. "I'll deal with Corby later," he said in a fierce voice, as he handed Gina her mask.

She sucked in her breath. "Yes, sir, Captain, sir!" Anyone overhearing them would automatically assume she was being chastised on the spot by her superior. With cheeks blazing red beneath the grime and soot, she left Grady to his job of filling in the incident report and went back downstairs. She scanned the fire ground for Lieutenant Corby and saw him standing by engine 1. Apparently Grady was now in command of ladder 1. Joining the others in the process of cleaning up, she walked over to help Winn, who was bringing down the extension. A man with a video camera sporting the Channel 8 logo intercepted her.

"I'd like to interview you for a minute, if I could?"

"Ask him." Gina nodded toward Winn. "He lifted a victim from the fourth floor down a fifty-five-foot extension ladder without being able to see an inch in front of him."

The cameraman scratched his head. "But somebody said a wo—"

"You'll have to clear the area." Grady's voice broke in. "My crew has a lot of cleanup work to do. You could get hurt."

Gina looked at Grady standing there in full turnout gear with his hands on his hips and couldn't imagine anyone defying him. To her relief, he seemed fully recovered and ready for action. The cameraman backed off and went elsewhere for a story while Gina helped Winn with the ladder.

The crew worked in silence. Back at the station when everyone relaxed, the men loved to chat, but on the job, Gina noticed that most of them didn't talk.

They simply went about their work in a methodical, orderly manner, unlike a lot of women she'd met, who needed to dissect and discuss every step of the way. Gina enjoyed the difference.

She avoided looking at Grady, and grew more uneasy after they all climbed into the truck and headed back to the station. She purposely scooted in next to Rico and practised her high school Spanish with him in an effort to expend some of her excess energy. Rico had an entertaining personality and kept things light. That prevented her from thinking about the inevitable moment when Grady would tell her she'd been assigned somewhere else for her next shift. She could feel the vibrations coming from him even though Winn sat between them.

Much to her relief, another call sent them out to contain a fire near the airport. It was after ten at night before both the engine and the ladder finally pulled into the station. Everyone was ravenous and stormed the kitchen.

Gina decided this was the best time to take her shower. Her real motive was to stay out of Grady's way. So far her plan to go nice and easy had backfired. She hadn't counted on the torrent of emotions his nearness evoked, and it appeared that her entry into his world had upset him so much he couldn't wait to be rid of her.

Turning off the taps, Gina reached for a towel and stepped from the shower just as the bathroom door opened.

"Grady!" she cried out in shock, hurriedly wrapping the towel around her body. But she hadn't been quick enough to escape the intimate appraisal of his eyes. "I—I thought the door was locked. I *know* I locked it!"

His gaze traveled once more over her silvery-gold hair still wet from a shampoo and came to rest on the little pulse that pounded mercilessly in the scented hollow of her throat. He closed the door, sealing them off from the others.

"How many times has this happened before?" His eyes were mere slits but she saw a telltale flush on his cheeks.

"This is the first. I swear it," she replied. He didn't say anything, though he made no move to leave. "I thought I'd shower while everyone ate. I always pick a time when I think it's safe, but for some reason, the lock didn't engage. I don't know why." Her voice trailed off because she had the impression he wasn't listening.

"This could cost you your badge."

"It was an accident, Grady." Her skin flamed with the heat of embarrassment and anger.

"If I didn't know we'd had trouble with this lock before, I'd think you were being deliberately provocative."

Her jaw clenched. "You know me better than that!"

"I thought I did," he ground out, sounding breathless. "If any other man had walked in here tonight and had seen what I saw—" He broke off. Gina looked away. "While you're at station 1, you'll refrain from showering or bathing on the premises, and that's an order."

She hitched the towel a little higher and glanced over at him. "I know what you must think but—"

"You haven't the slightest idea," he fired back. Gina's violet eyes played over his face. It had an unnatural pallor and his eyelids drooped. He shouldn't have come back to work this soon. He hadn't fully recovered from his earlier ordeal, she realized now. Compassion for the man she loved made her want to hold out her arms and enfold him. Instead, she averted her eyes.

"If you'll excuse me, I'll get dressed and go to bed," she muttered.

"Before I go I want your promise about not showering."

"You have it." She swallowed hard. "Grady? You don't look well," she said impulsively. "Why didn't you stay home for a few more days?"

He drew in his breath and reached for the doorknob. "It's a good thing I didn't, wouldn't you say? Corby's panting for an opportunity just like this."

"You've made your point, Grady."

"I haven't even started," he growled and left the bathroom. She heard the lock click as he closed the door behind him.

For a moment, the bathroom seemed to tilt and Gina gripped the edge of the sink with both hands. She didn't blame Grady. The coincidence of his walking in just then, of the lock slipping at that very moment, was almost too improbable to believe.

She bit her lip in an effort to stem the tears. Of all the stupid things to have happened, this was the worst. Grady was an extremely private person. This kind of situation could only offend him—the last thing she wanted to do.

The gong sounded for engine 1 and she threw on her clothes, only to be waylaid by Grady as she opened the door. Apparently he wasn't taking any chances on that lock. "Frank's filling in on this assist," he said coldly. "I want you to go to bed, and I suggest you go there now!"

It was on the tip of her tongue to take issue with his orders, but the angry look in his eye made her reconsider. Without a word, she walked through the station to his dimly lit office and lay down on the bunk, her heart pounding hard. As soon as the engine had left the bay, Grady appeared in the room. He shut the door, and for what seemed like an eternity he stood there, not saying anything.

She couldn't stand the silence any longer. "Am I being punished—sent to my room?"

"Gang fights are no place for a woman, and I wouldn't care if you held ten black belts in karate. One jab of a stiletto in a vulnerable spot could mean a permanent disability."

Gina sat up, tucking her legs beneath her. "You told me at my apartment that you were going to treat me exactly like the others."

"I intended to until you broke all the rules."

She tossed her head. "The Grady I used to know knew how to forgive—particularly an unavoidable accident."

Even in the half-light, she could feel the menace in his expression. "Apparently the job has brought out a dark side in both of us."

"That's not true, Grady." Her voice trembled. "I'm sorry for what happened earlier. Can't we let it go at that?"

"Once again, you're asking the impossible, Gina."

"Oh, for heaven's sake, Grady. We used to be married. It isn't as if you haven't seen me in the shower before. Naturally I'm thankful it was you who happened to walk in on me. If it had been anyone else, I would have died of embarrassment."

She heard a noise come out of him that sounded like ripping silk. "I thought you did a fairly convincing imitation of embarrassment when I walked in. As many times as you've blushed in my arms, I've never seen you look quite that . . . disturbed before."

Gina sank back on the mattress and turned her head away from him. "I don't want to think about it anymore."

"So help me, I don't want to think about it, either," he whispered. Abruptly he paced several steps and when he spoke again, his voice was brisk. "You'll ride ladder the rest of the shift."

"Yes, sir."

"Gina?"

"What else have I done wrong?" she asked, sighing wearily.

"Confine your hair to a ponytail while you're on duty. Don't flaunt your beauty in front of the men. Corby lost it this morning when you arrived for work. He's angry because you rebuffed him in front of everyone at the condo. That's why he assigned you to ladder."

"I know." She heaved another sigh. "He phoned me at the apartment, but I didn't return his call and I guess that added fuel to the fire."

"To your credit, the crew is recommending you for a medal for that rescue today, which will only make Corby more determined to get even with you. Be careful, Gina."

"What more can I do? I've told him point-blank I don't date fire fighters."

"Just being who you are is problem enough," he murmured enigmatically. "Stay out of his way until Whittaker gets back."

She raised herself up on one elbow. "You're making me out to be some kind of femme fatale." She laughed nervously.

"Come off it, Gina. You've always been a knockout, and you know it. If anything, the turnout gear emphasizes your femininity. There's nothing you can do about the way nature made you, but for the good of the station, try not to draw undue attention to yourself."

"Maybe I should get my hair cut."

"Unfortunately that wouldn't change a thing."

The fact that he still found her attractive should have thrilled her, but his voice sounded ragged and she couldn't stop worrying about his physical condition. "You're tired, Grady. Why not lie down and rest?"

"Is that an invitation, Gina?" he mocked in that hateful manner.

"Would you like it to be?" she taunted, after a long silence.

He swore softly, then wheeled from the room. His abrupt departure pleased her. The idea that Grady wasn't as much in control as he'd led her to believe brought a satisfied smile to her lips. There'd been no need for him to follow her back to his office. He'd instigated this last conversation as if he hadn't been able to help himself.

She turned onto her stomach and hugged the pillow. It was the first sign that maybe, just maybe, she was getting under his skin. In fact, she'd begun to think that lasting this long at station 1 was a miracle in itself.

CHAPTER FOUR

TENNIS AND SWIMMING were Gina's favorite ways of keeping in shape, but some of those activities had to be curtailed during the next week to make time for singing rehearsals. She would be taking part in the entertainment at the annual Fire Fighters' Ball.

Nancy Byington, a fire fighter from station 5, had been made cochair of the ball, and she was out to revolutionize what had always been an event sponsored by the men and their wives. Nancy's reputation as a pioneer in forging the way for more female fire fighters preceded her. When Gina received a call from Nancy asking for help, she was delighted to oblige, particularly as the ball was being held at the soon-to-close Hotel Olympus.

Besides being in charge of the intermission activities, Nancy planned to emcee the dance and to force people to mingle and get to know one another. Her plan to remove a few barriers was met with enthusiasm by other veterans in the department. Preball publicity infiltrated all the stations, urging everyone to attend, with or without a partner. This was one event in which all personnel were expected to participate.

The foyer of the famous old hotel had been transformed into a palace garden. Three-tiered topiary trees strung with thousands of tiny white lights, interspersed with baskets of roses and petunias, created a magical mood, enhanced by the magnificent crystal chandelier shimmering above the marble dance floor below. Nancy jokingly told Gina and the others taking part in the entertainment that they wanted to bring down the house, but "please *not* the chandelier."

On one side of the raised platform where the intermission activities would be performed were the buffet tables. Enough room had been left on the other side to accommodate the orchestra. The tables bordering the dance floor had been reserved for VIPs within the various departments, as well as visiting dignitaries in state and local government.

As the time approached for intermission, Gina looked down from her vantage point on the mezzanine floor. The group was highly animated, encouraged, no doubt, by Nancy's guidance. So far, they'd done a conga line, a Virginia reel, break dancing for the more daring, a waltz for all people more than fifty and a fox-trot for everyone between forty and fifty. The list of innovative ways to get everyone involved went on and on. And all the while, Gina's eyes had been searching for Grady. So far she hadn't seen him. Maybe he'd decided not to come, and stayed on at the station with the skeleton crew.

"Can't you find him?" Susan asked in a low voice. She was the only person in the department who knew about Grady.

"Not yet."

"Will I do?"

Gina turned around and began to laugh, and the sound caught the attention of the other two female fire fighters. The four of them were dressed like male fire fighters, in turnout coats and pants several sizes too large to accommodate their evening gowns. In gloves, air masks and helmets pulled down to disguise their hair, no one would know they were women. They stood tall in their huge boots, since they were wearing high heels. So far, no one had any idea who they were.

With a great deal of difficulty, they moved down the staircase and walked out onto the platform when Nancy gave the signal. A ripple of laughter started among the audience and began to build as they approached the microphone. Gina could hear several boisterous asides telling them to go back to the station.

Her heart started to run away with her as she quickly scanned the audience now seated at tables to watch the floor show. Several hundred salaried fire fighters and volunteers, with their partners, were assembled, wearing tuxedos and evening gowns. It was when she looked beneath the overhang where she'd been standing before the show that she saw Grady with a good-looking brunette sparkling up at him. As Grady was one of the VIPs, he sat at a table near the buffet and dance floor, so close she could detect his slightly bored smile. He looked devastatingly handsome, but not nearly as animated as his date. A duty affair like this was not his favorite activity, and she had an idea he'd only come for appearance's sake. How Gina longed to wipe that world-weary expression from his face. Frank sat at Grady's table with a petite redhead. A few tables away she saw Howard and Ed with their wives. No matter how hard Nancy tried to force people to mix, the men tended to stick together.

"Since you guys gate-crashed this party, you're going to have to sing for your supper," Nancy began her introduction as the lights dimmed and the spotlight came on to blind the performers. "What do you say, audience?"

A huge cheer went up from the crowd.

"All right, Firebrands. Take it away!"

Someone behind the scenes started the tape recorder and the women lipsynched and mimed their way through "Smoke Gets in Your Eyes," "Ring of Fire" and "Heat Wave."

The choice of songs was a huge success. When the singers finished, the men in the audience got to their feet and clapped for three minutes. A fire fighter planted in the crowd shouted, "We want to hear what they really sound like!" This brought on a chorus of shouts and joking.

"So you want the real thing, do you?" Nancy's voice rang out.

"Yes!" the audience responded.

"All right. But remember! You asked for it!" When Nancy turned to the women, it was their cue to disrobe. Synchronizing their actions, they removed their helmets, masks and gloves, undid their turnout coats and pants, kicked off their boots and wriggled out of everything to step forward dressed in crimson chiffon, calf-length evening gowns. "The Firebrands," Nancy said, motioning them closer to the microphone.

The clapping and whistling started. The men were on their feet once more. No one had guessed who'd been hidden beneath the turnout gear. The quick-change-artist routine was an unqualified success, and it took time for everyone to quiet down.

"I'm going to ask each of the women to step forward as I say her name and identify her station," Nancy continued. "Believe it or not, these ladies are some of the intrepid fire fighters protecting our city. Station 7's representative is Karen Slogowski, station 5's is Susan Orr, station 4, Mavis Carr and, last but not least, from our famous station 1, representing Grady's bunch—Gina Lindsay."

Pandemonium broke out with more cheering and clapping. Finally it subsided as the group began singing to a recorded background music tape of the Beach Boys' hit, "Kokomo." Gina's voice supplied first alto, and for a bunch of amateurs, she felt they performed rather well. The song was a favorite and the long applause at the end of the number reflected the crowd's approval.

"All right, folks. You've heard from the Firebrands. Now we're going to have them bring back the dancing by starting out with Ladies' Choice. Now, confidentially," Nancy told the audience, "our performers haven't rehearsed this part of the program. In fact, they have no idea what's going to happen next."

A hush fell over Gina and the others. Susan's eyebrows quirked while Gina held her breath, wondering what Nancy was about to pull. She wasn't the emcee for nothing!

"You know," Nancy continued, "these ladies take a lot of orders from their superiors day in and day out. I think it would be kind of nice to turn the tables for a change. Where are the captains of these personifications of courage and pulchritude? Come on—stand up! That's an order! Let's have the lights on."

While pandemonium reigned once more, Gina felt faint and flashed a distress signal at Susan, who winked conspiratorially. Gina suspected Susan was behind this, but could do absolutely nothing about it as the glittering chandelier illuminated the room.

"Ladies, go find your captains and let the dancing begin! And all you wives and sweethearts out there, once these four have taken a twirl around the dance floor, it's your turn to pick a new partner and *mingle*!" When Nancy finished her spiel, Sue whispered to Gina that this was her chance.

Flushed with a feverish excitement, Gina made her way slowly across the gleaming marble floor toward Grady. On the periphery, she could see the other women approaching their captains, who stood up amid continued cheering and joking, awaiting their fate. The orchestra had started to play a bossa nova number that lighted a fire in her blood. What was meant to be simply good fun had turned into something else, at least for Gina. The realization that within seconds she'd be in Grady's strong arms caused a tremor to rock her body.

Grady's eyes ignited to a quicksilver color as she drew closer. His unsmiling gaze roamed over her face and hair, then fell lower to the curves swathed in crimson chiffon, and lower still to her jeweled high-heeled sandals sparkling like the diamond earrings she wore—the ones he'd given her for a wedding present.

She'd brushed her hair till it gleamed white-gold and curved under her chin from a center part. She wore a peach lip gloss and a touch of lavender eye shadow that matched the deeper violet irises. Not even on her wedding night had she wanted to look as beautiful for Grady as she did now. Her cheeks needed no blusher. Hectic color made her skin hot, and she had difficulty breathing as she finally stopped in front of him.

Other people were at the table, but it seemed to her that a nimbus surrounded Grady, blotting out everyone else. He stood tall and straight, like a prince—magnificent in black with a pearly-gray cummerbund, which matched his crystalline eyes. His indecently long black lashes gave them their particular incandescent quality. For a brief moment his expression sent out a message of sensual awareness that Gina felt to the depths of her being.

"Captain Simpson? May I have this dance?"

His half smile was a slash of white in his bronzed face. "What would you do if I said no?" he asked, his voice mocking, and her heart began to knock in her breast. Nervously, she moistened her glistening lips.

"Then I guess I'd have to ask your second in command."

She'd said it teasingly, but a dull flush suddenly tinged his cheeks as he gathered her in his arms and swung her out onto the dance floor.

During their marriage, their bodies had been so perfectly attuned, that even now Gina's hand slid automatically toward his neck. Then, when she remembered where they were, she quickly moved it to his broad shoulder, in a clumsy, betraying motion. His chest heaved as if he, too, had momentarily gone back in time. In Cairo they'd danced the nights away during their brief honeymoon. Right now, it seemed the most natural thing in the world for Gina to melt against him and make a kind of slow-motion love to him as they danced.... But of course they couldn't do that in sight of hundreds of people—including his date for the evening.

As if by tacit agreement, Grady circled her around the floor at a discreet distance, while other couples started to join in. Gina happened to be wearing Grady's favorite French perfume, and that, combined with the male tang of his body and the hint of musk he wore, intoxicated her. Her eyes were level with his chin where she saw a little telltale nerve throbbing madly near the tiny scar at the corner of his mouth. Whatever his feelings were for her at this point, her nearness disturbed him. She'd been married to him too long not to know the signs. This response of his was something to cherish.

"It's sinful how beautiful you are," he grated, and her eyes flashed upward, in confusion—and hope. For an unguarded moment his eyes blazed with the old hunger that made her knees go weak.

"I could tell you the same thing," she whispered in a husky voice, not realizing she was caressing the palm of his hand with her thumb until she heard his quick intake of breath and felt the pressure of his hand forcing her to stop the teasing motion. "I'm sorry."

He didn't pretend to misunderstand her. "It comes as naturally to you as breathing, doesn't it, Gina?"

The censure in his tone caused her to stiffen and she almost missed her step. "What do you mean?"

"You're a born temptress. The first time I saw you, you flashed those incredible violet eyes at me and I fell a thousand feet without knowing what in the hell had hit me."

She swallowed hard. "I—I felt the same way. You were bigger than life."

"For a little while, we tasted paradise," he murmured with a tinge of sadness in his deep voice, "but apparently it wasn't meant to be a steady diet." He cocked his dark head to the side. "Is that what your floor show was all about? A trip down memory lane?" His smile was more cynical than anything else and didn't reach his eyes. "If so, you succeeded admirably."

His words made her spirits plummet sharply. He might have been in love with her once, but no longer. Searing pain almost immobilized her as she understood what he was telling her—it was too late....

"This whole thing may have looked contrived, but Nancy spoke the truth. Dancing with our captains was her idea. She's determined to promote better relations between the men and the women. She had no way of knowing how...abhorrent it would be to you."

There was a long pause, then, "Never abhorrent, Gina. You're the stuff men's dreams are made of, didn't you know?"

But not your dreams, she agonized inwardly. "I think we've danced long enough to satisfy protocol. Your date will be waiting."

Grady stopped dancing even though the orchestra still played. A strange tension emanated from him. "Where's your date? I'll deliver you back to him."

Ever the gentleman...but his offer had the effect of plunging a dagger in her heart. She would have loved to produce such a person for him, but she'd come alone and would go home alone. She found she couldn't lie to him. "Those of us performing didn't have dates. We need to be on hand to clean up after everything's over. Have a nice evening, Captain Simpson," she whispered, unable to look up at him. If she hadn't known better, she would have thought he let go of her arms reluctantly as she slipped away and moved across the crowded floor toward the buffet. At the moment she desperately needed a cold glass of punch.

Once again Nancy's voice sounded through the mike, announcing that the next dance was for people without partners. Gina grimaced at the irony and swallowed the rest of her punch.

"Do I dare ask for a dance?" The familiar voice came from directly behind her.

"Lieutenant Corby," Gina finally acknowledged him, surprising an unexpected look of contrition shining out of his light blue eyes.

"I did a dumb thing the other day, assigning you to ladder, and I'd like to apologize."

Gina folded her arms. "I'm certified to ride ladder, Bob. No apologies are necessary."

"I know." He nodded, and there was a moment's uncharacteristic hesitation. "It's my reasons for doing it that I'd like to explain."

Gina took a deep breath. "Did the captain ask you to?"

He looked affronted. "We exchanged a few words, but this apology is my own idea." Something in his tone forced Gina to believe him. "I don't usually have trouble getting a woman to go out with me." He scratched his ear. "I know that sounds conceited, but it's true."

"I can believe it," she interjected good-naturedly.

He stared at her for a moment. "It ticked me off that I couldn't get to first base with you. In fact, I'm still having a hard time seeing you as one of the crew."

"You and all the others." She smiled.

He shook his head. "No...some of the guys are further along than I am. I guess I just don't want to fight fires with a woman. There are a lot of other things I'd rather do with her." He grinned.

"I admire your honesty. I suppose if a man started coming to my all-female sewing club, I'd feel uncomfortable about it myself."

His brows quirked. "That's not the best analogy I've ever heard."

Gina laughed. "I know, but I can't think of a better one. Women fire fighters are unprecedented—"

"Particularly ones who look like you," he broke in. "I thought Captain Simpson was immune, judging by the way he's treated you at the station, but after tonight, I can see he's as vulnerable as the rest of us."

"He was ordered to dance with me," she retorted to cover the sudden fluttering of her pulse.

His lips twitched. "Would it take an order to get you out on that dance floor now? I purposely didn't bring a date because I hoped you'd take pity on me." His hands lifted in a gesture of comical despair. "I promise this won't obligate you to anything else."

"Sure, why not?" she answered and allowed him to guide her onto the floor.

"Do you samba?" The orchestra was doing a whole series of Latin dance numbers. Gina nodded. "All right, then."

Bob Corby turned out to be an accomplished dancer, challenging Gina's ability to keep up with him. The first dance was over so soon that he begged for another. Soon Gina forgot to count. She hadn't had this good a time in ages. She'd have the rest of the night—the rest of her life—to torture herself with thoughts of Grady and all she'd lost.

She purposely kept her attention on Bob so she wouldn't be tempted to stare at Grady. But when he suddenly gripped Bob's shoulder during their last dance, Gina was forced to meet gray eyes as dark as storm clouds. Why he should look that angry she had no idea. Dancing with Bob didn't constitute high treason, nor did it mean she'd accept a date with him. She'd already made that promise to Grady, so she couldn't understand what kind of feelings could produce such hostile emotion.

"Captain?" Bob turned to him with the same happy smile he'd been wearing as they danced. "Are you trying to cut in on me?" Gina could hear the crackle of the walkie-talkie.

Something flickered in the recesses of Grady's eyes. "We're all needed back at the station. A tire warehouse was set on fire by arsonists. They're calling for additional units. Did you both bring cars?" They nodded.

Even as he spoke, she could see various crews walking away from the tables. It was amazing the ball had gone as long as it had without interruption.

"Gina?" He used her first name, which was a shock. "You'll ride back to the station with me. Someone can help you collect your car later." Gina felt too surprised to respond.

"I'll meet you there, Captain." Bob was all business now and took off at a run.

Gina wondered what had happened to Grady's date, but experienced a sudden, unholy surge of joy that he wouldn't be spending the rest of the night in the other woman's arms. She wouldn't allow herself to dwell on the pictures that immediately filled her mind.

Gina ran to keep up with Grady as they took a side exit and raced down two levels to the underground car park where he'd left the Audi. He helped her in before coming around to the driver's side and starting the engine. With the economy of movement she'd always admired, he backed out and they were off to the station, less than a mile away.

"In case you're wondering why I insisted you come with me, I thought this might be my only opportunity to talk to you privately before we go off duty."

"If this is about Lieutenant Corby, I've already told you I don't date fire fighters."

"I believe you, Gina, but I want to give you a warning. Corby's been bragging to the guys that he's going to have you in bed by the time Whittaker returns to duty."

She rubbed her forehead, where she could feel the beginnings of a headache. "Well, he can brag all he wants. His boast is meaningless," she said disgustedly.

Grady's hands tightened on the steering wheel, his knuckles turning white. "You and I may know it's pure fantasy, but the crew is another matter altogether, and your dancing with him all night adds credence. Once a rumor starts, it can fly out of control and no amount of truth can set it right."

"Are you telling me you're worried about my reputation?" she asked in amazement.

"I'm worried about problems with my crew, Gina. When a crack forms in the foundation, the whole place can come crashing down if you're not careful. We were all getting along fine—"

"Until I came to replace Whittaker." She finished the words for him. "It's no longer a mystery why you wanted this little tête-à-tête. Is this your polite way of getting me to bow out gracefully? Am I supposed to do the noble thing?"

Grady literally stood on his brakes as the car pulled into the parking area behind the station. He jerked his head around and glared at her. "Do you know a better way? Corby has seven years' seniority over you."

"And would bring a nasty lawsuit against you if you had him switched to another station for no good reason," she shot back bitterly. "But of course no one would expect me to bring a suit against him for sexual harassment, because women don't belong in the department to start with." Her eyes flashed purple in the dim interior. "Nancy's right. This department still lives in the dark ages!" On that note she got out of the car and slammed the door before she could hear Grady's response.

"Gina?" he called after her, slamming his own door. He ran to catch up with her. "I'm not through with you." He reached out and grabbed her arm, closing his hand over soft, warm flesh.

She whirled around, causing the chiffon to swing lovingly around her long, shapely legs. "Is that an order, Captain?" The blood was pounding in her temples, and her diamond earrings glittered with every heartbeat.

Grady's face had lost some of its color, and his mouth thinned into an uncompromising line of aggression. But before he could say anything else, they both heard the sound of the back door opening. Grady let go of her arm as if her skin had scalded him. "It's the captain!" one of the crew shouted. "Let's get ready to roll."

Gina wasted no time hurrying inside and changing into her coveralls and boots.

"You forgot something," Bob muttered as they all dived for their turnout coats on the hooks in the bay.

"What?" she asked almost impatiently, growing more and more resentful of Bob for being the cause of the latest confrontation between her and Grady.

"These." His fingers reached into the silken strands of her hair and removed the earrings. "They look real enough that I'd hate to see you lose them." The brazen gesture suggested an intimacy they didn't share. To her consternation, Grady had witnessed the byplay. There was a murderous gleam in his eyes that reminded her of their conversation in the car. His furious glance reiterated his earlier accusation—that her mere presence created a problem. And worse—it brought to mind the night Grady had given her those earrings. Now was not the time to recall those hours of ecstasy. . . .

Gina took her earrings from Bob without saying anything and put them in one of her pockets. Earlier in the evening she'd been prepared to forget any friction and make a friend of him, but no longer. Unfortunately, he was her superior on the engine, which meant spending the rest of the shift in his company.

Other units were already battling the blaze when Gina's engine pulled up to the fire ground. Bob ordered Gina to lead in with the hose and start spraying the exterior of the warehouse to reduce the temperatures for the men on ladders. Ed worked with her, anticipating her movements as they carried the unwieldy hose across the crowded pavement surrounding the building.

Black smoke billowed from the roof, filling the air with hot fumes that burned her lungs. The place was a roaring inferno, singeing her brows and lashes as she trained the powerful spray on the wall of flame threatening the man above her on the ladder. At times she could scarcely see a foot in front of her.

When she heard a shout coming from somewhere overhead, she lifted her face instinctively. And that was the moment something glanced off her helmet, knocking her into oblivion.

"SHE'S COMING AROUND. Other than a gigantic headache, I think she's going to be okay."

Gina was cognizant of several things at once. Cool fresh air was being forced into her starving lungs and she could hear voices around her, one of them Grady's.

She pushed the mask away from her face and opened her eyes to discover she was inside an ambulance. She immediately focused on Grady's blackened face, but what impressed her most was the look of pain in his eyes.

"Don't move, Gina. Just lie still and take it easy."

She couldn't understand why he was there. "What happened? I heard a noise and suddenly everything went black."

He closed his eyes tightly for a minute, apparently held in the grip of some intense emotion. "A man from ladder 3 was overcome and his hose slipped," Grady started to explain. "His backup man braced to keep the hose from snaking, but you were standing in its path." His voice shook. "We can thank God it was only the hose and not the nozzle that sent you flying."

She sighed. A full hose running under pressure could break bones, or worse. "Sorry to leave you a man short, Captain." She gave Grady a wan smile.

"Gina..." he whispered in an agonized voice. She'd never heard Grady sound like that before and warmth surged through her heart, quickening her entire body. She no longer felt any pain. Somewhere deep inside him he still had feelings. Feelings for her. The knowledge caused her eyes to fill with tears. She blinked them away.

"You shouldn't be here, Captain. I'm fine. How's the other guy?"

His eyes played over her features for a long moment before he spoke, as if he were having trouble getting his emotions under control. His vulnerability was a revelation to Gina. Did he have any idea how hard he was squeezing her hand?

"I don't know," he finally answered in a thick voice. "We'll find out when we get to Emergency."

"I heard the attendant tell you I was going to be okay."

"You are." His relief was undisguised. "But I want an X ray to find out if you've suffered a concussion."

Gina moved her head tentatively. It was sore at the crown. "I don't feel sick to my stomach. I think that's a pretty good indication it's not serious. Are my pupils still dilated?"

An epithet escaped his taut lips. "You know too much for your own good."

Her smile was impish. "Does that annoy you?"

Her question seemed to catch him off guard. "Do you want the truth?"

"Nothing but."

"I prefer to think of you the way you were a few hours ago, but I'll confess that you're a good fire fighter, with more courage than I've seen in a number of men."

"That's high praise indeed coming from the illustrious Captain Grady."

With that remark his expression sobered. "Whatever the prognosis once we get to the hospital, you're exempted from duty for a while."

Her eyes searched his for reasons. "Why?"

"To give you a chance to fully recover—and to cool an explosive situation with Corby."

Gina ran a shaky hand through her hair. Grady still held on to the other, and it seemed completely natural. "What he did back at the station was inexcusable."

He sucked in his breath. "In all fairness to him, what he did he couldn't help. You're pretty well irresistible to the male of the species, Gina."

"Loyal to your male crew to the bitter end, aren't you, Grady."

"Realistic," he retorted solemnly. "All eyes were on you at the hotel. They couldn't help but be anywhere else. Men are the weaker sex, didn't you know that? Your smile can twist a man into knots and have him begging for more. Corby's no different from any other man in that regard."

"And he's the best fire fighter in the city next to you."

His dark brows furrowed. "He's *one* of the best."

But if it were a choice between her and Lieutenant Corby, Gina knew in her heart which one of them Grady would choose. There was no contest. Suddenly all the fight seemed to go out of her.

"Gina?" He sounded alarmed when he heard the small moan that escaped her lips. "Are you feeling ill?"

"I think I'm tired." Which was the truth, but more than that, she knew she'd lost the battle and the war. Grady couldn't have spelled it out any more plainly, and their conversation had the effect of numbing her.

"I shouldn't have allowed you to talk so long," he muttered.

"I'm glad you did. It's put everything into perspective." Her eyelids fluttered closed but not before she glimpsed the puzzled frown on his face, the uncertainty. It was a rare sight and one that would haunt her over the next few days.

CHAPTER FIVE

THE X RAY REVEALED a minor concussion, and Gina was ordered to bed for a few days. Sue and Nancy both came by the apartment several times to visit and help out. The guys at the station sent Gina a get-well card. All the signatures were there, including Grady's.

Bob called, leaving a message on the answering machine. He didn't press for a date. All he wanted was to wish her well; he also confessed that everyone missed her around station 1.

On her fourth day, she felt pretty much back to normal, except for an occasional headache. Anxious to be back on the job, she called the station and asked for Grady. If he didn't want her returning to his station, then she needed his permission to call headquarters and get reassigned. Someone she didn't know answered and said Captain Grady was off duty on his long weekend. Frustrated, Gina phoned Grady's condo. She didn't have to look up his number; he'd kept their old one. To her chagrin, he didn't answer and hadn't switched on his answering machine—if he even owned an answering machine. She didn't know.

At loose ends, she wandered out to the small patio off her dining room and lay down on the lounger to sunbathe. The heat was too intense to stay out for long, but it felt good.

She drank lemonade and listened to the radio. Reading still bothered her, but the doctor said that was a common side effect and would clear up in another day or two.

With one side of her body tinged a faint pink, she decided to turn over on her stomach and start tanning the backs of her legs. She closed her eyes, resting her head on her folded arms. She'd been lying in that position for only a few minutes when she felt a shadow fall over her. It was such a surprise, she jerked around and almost fell off the lounger. "Grady!"

"I'm sorry if I frightened you. I rang the front doorbell but I guess you didn't hear it."

She tugged the straps of her faded black one-piece bathing suit a little higher in a self-conscious gesture and switched off the radio. He stood there with his hands on his hips, legs slightly apart. No one looked better in a T-shirt and shorts than Grady. She swallowed hard and scrambled to her feet. "I—I'm glad you dropped by. I've been trying to reach you. Why don't we go inside? It's too hot out here."

Aware of his eyes on her, she almost ran into her bedroom for a toweling robe. Anything to cover herself. She ran a brush through her hair, willing her heart to stop pounding so hard. When she returned to the front room she found him planted in front of her photographs. Many were of him, in various situations; others showed the two of them together. If he found it odd that she still held on to them, he didn't say anything and she didn't explain.

He cast her a level glance over his shoulder. The mocking smile that tugged the corners of his mouth made her feel a need to hide behind her robe.

"Would you like some lemonade?" she asked hastily.

"Only if you don't go to a lot of trouble."

"It's already made."

He drew one bronzed hand through his dark hair. "You look too good for someone recovering from a concussion."

"I feel good. I still have a headache but it's slowly letting up." She hurried into the kitchen and poured them each a glass of lemonade. When she turned around, he was blocking the doorway, and his tall, lean frame seemed to dwarf her compact, tidy kitchen. There was something different about Grady—an intangible quality that stole the ground out from under her. All his pent-up anger seemed to be missing.

"I received the card. Tell everyone thank-you." She handed him a glass, which he took and immediately drained then held out for a refill. The action reminded her so much of the old days she broke into a full-bodied smile, which miraculously he reciprocated.

"The card was Frank's contribution. I think he's gone into mourning that you're not around."

"He's not the only one." She poured the last drop of lemonade from the pitcher into Grady's glass and handed it back. "I'm not used to this much inactivity and I'm going a little stir-crazy."

His devastating smile faded to be replaced by a more serious expression. "That's what I came over to talk to you about—and, of course, to see if you were feeling better."

She tucked a loose strand of hair behind her ear with unconscious allure. "As you can see, I'm fine and eager to get back to work."

He stared hard at her as he finished his second drink. "How would you like to take a drive up into the mountains for the rest of the day? It'll give you a break from this enforced idleness. And we'll have a chance to discuss your future with the department."

His last statement sounded ominous, but the joy she experienced at his invitation superseded all other thoughts. She had to fight to control her reactions. She hadn't seen Grady this mellow since long before the divorce and didn't want to do anything to disturb this momentary truce. "I—I'd love to get out of this heat. Do you mind if I take a quick shower first?"

For the merest fraction of a second, their eyes met in shared remembrance of the countless times he'd joined her there as a prelude to something else equally consuming and intimate. When she realized where her thoughts had wandered, she looked away. Grady shifted his weight as if he, too, had to make a determined effort to keep those memories in the past.

"Take all the time you need. I'll wait for you in the car."

She nodded. "I'll hurry."

Less than ten minutes later, she joined Grady. She'd dressed carefully, choosing white linen shorts and a lavender-blue crocheted top that fit at the waist and had puffed sleeves. A white silk scarf kept the hair out of her eyes as the Audi's open sunroof let in an exhilarating breeze.

Gina had little inclination to talk and apparently Grady felt the same way. When they entered Parley's Canyon for the steep climb to the summit, she was flooded by a bittersweet sense of déjà vu. They'd traveled this section of highway so many times in the past, on their way to picnics in the mountains. The tantalizing scent of his musk after-shave blended with the refreshing aroma of pine, and it took her back to those exquisite early days when they could hardly bear to be apart, even for an hour or two.

"I don't know about you but I'm hungry," he said as he took the turnoff for Midway, their favorite spot.

"So am I. Are you in the mood for hamburgers or pizza?"

"Actually, I had a picnic in mind. It's packed in the trunk."

Gina's eyes widened in amazement. "I haven't been on a picnic s—in a long time," she amended, struggling to keep her composure. Like a revelation, it came to her that he'd planned this outing. She couldn't help but wonder where he was taking them and could hardly breathe from excitement.

The back side of Timpanogos Mountain with its snow-crested peaks dominated the Swiss-like countryside. Gina felt a piercingly sweet ache of such longing, she was afraid to look at Grady. This was one time she couldn't disguise her emotions.

He was strangely silent as he drove through the tiny hamlet of Midway, past the post office. When he suddenly turned the corner and stopped in front of her favorite red-and-white gingerbread house—a type of architecture for which Midway was famous—she didn't understand. The little house with its pointed roof and lacy white scrollwork peered out from four giant blue spruce trees, like some enchanted cottage in the Black Forest. The lawn was a velvety spring green, and the white fence looked freshly painted.

Gina turned to Grady. "Are we going to have our picnic *here*?" she asked incredulously.

His smile was mysterious. "Every time we went past this house, you told me you wanted to have a picnic under those trees. Today I'm granting you your wish."

Her cry of joy could not be restrained. "Did you arrange this with the owners?"

"I did," he affirmed, as he levered himself out of the car. Gina jumped from her side and gazed all around at the magnificent view of the mountains surrounding them. She thought she might die of happiness to have Grady all to herself in this paradise. Her ecstatic glance darted to him.

"Let me help." She reached in the trunk for the blanket while he lifted out the basket of food, then she followed him through the little gate to a nest of spruce needles beneath the largest tree. Gina spread out the blanket and they sat down, reveling in the cool shade.

"Are the people away? How did you manage it?" She threw him one question after another as he began to fill her plate with chicken and potato salad. She, in turn, opened a bottle of sparkling white wine he'd provided and poured it into paper cups, sneaking a taste.

Grady sat cross-legged, munching on a drumstick. "I own it, Gina," he said matter-of-factly. Her motions abrupt, she put down the wine bottle, her violet eyes searching his for what seemed a timeless moment. "About six months after our divorce became final, my realtor called me and told me it had finally come on the market. I told him to start the paperwork immediately."

Tears came to her eyes unbidden. This little house had been their dream—their fantasy. To think that all this time, he'd been the owner, had taken care of it, lived in it, *without her*.

The wine no longer tasted sweet.

Grady blinked when he saw that she wasn't eating. He wiped the edge of his mouth with a napkin. "What's wrong, Gina? Are you feeling ill?"

"No." She shook her head and looked down. "I'm just surprised the people would sell it. You'd think a family would want to keep it for generations to come."

"The man who owned it died without leaving any heirs."

"You must have been thrilled," she said, studying her nails.

Grady looked pensive. "It's just a house, Gina. A place I come to relax and write—when I can find the time."

She hugged her arms to her chest. "The place looks immaculate."

"I have a caretaker who does odd jobs and house-sits when I'm not here. So far, the arrangement has worked out well."

As far as Gina could tell, Grady's bachelor life-style suited him perfectly. He had no need for permanent entanglements, no romantic notions to complicate his well-ordered existence. Had he brought her up here to demonstrate just how smoothly he'd made the transition from bondage to freedom? She hadn't suspected he had a deliberately cruel side.

"Would you like to come inside and have a look around? I bought it furnished because I haven't had the time to take on a redecorating project."

"Of course I'd like to see it." She rose to her feet and accompanied Grady up the walk to the front porch with its old-fashioned swing. The interior of the house had the makings of a turn-of-the-century museum, from a grandfather clock to a cane-backed rocking chair by the hearth. With a few improvements, it could be a veritable showplace.

Grady had turned the parlor into a den. While he sorted through a pile of manuscripts, Gina went upstairs to survey the two quaint bedrooms. Each window had a view of the mountains. The house was as adorable inside as it was out. And Grady owned it!

Gina felt as if someone had played a cruel trick on her. She'd been allowed a glimpse of paradise before it was gone from sight forever. "Does the reality live up to the fantasy?" Gina hadn't heard him come up the stairs and frantically brushed away the tears with the back of her hand.

"I think you already know the answer to that question." Her voice shook. "Can I ask you one?"

"Fire away."

"Why did you bring me here?"

She could feel the warmth of his body and knew he couldn't be standing more than a few inches away.

"I wanted to talk to you in a favorable ambience—away from everyone else—where we could communicate for once, instead of hurling abuse at each other."

She bowed her head, acknowledging his reasons. For so long their marriage had been little more than a battleground. She had to reach far back to remember times like this. "You didn't need to go to such elaborate lengths to soften me, Grady. I know I'm a complication you can't wait to be rid of." She took a deep breath. "I called you this morning to tell you I'm willing to take the next available posting, if that's what you want. It's not necessary for me to be at station 1. Whether you believe me or not, I find no joy in coming between you and your men. Grady's bunch is legendary, you know."

She expected anything but the dark silence that followed her statement.

"I told you in the ambulance that you do good work, Gina," he finally said. "Another station will be lucky to get you, and I mean that sincerely. I'll make it clear on the transfer that the reason for the change is due to Whittaker's return. He'll be back a week from Monday. Your time at the station has only been cut by four days as it is. We can get by with three men on the engine crew for that short a time.''

She rubbed her arms as if she were cold. ''Then I'll call headquarters in the morning.''

''I understand station 6 needs a paramedic. It's a quieter station, not so many runs. You'd be happy there.''

Heat filled her cheeks as she whirled around. ''I prefer heavier action, Grady. The more runs, the better.''

He frowned, the lines marring his handsome face. ''The risk of danger takes a quantum leap in a station like number 1. You're still recovering from a concussion. You'd be a fool to go back for more of the same,'' he said, his voice strained now as the tension began to build.

Her jaw stiffened. ''I remember telling you the same thing when we were married.''

He gave a short, angry laugh. ''I'm a man, Gina. Don't try making comparisons.''

''So we're back to that again. For your information, *I* was out there doing my job when a *man* lost his hose and I got the brunt of it.''

''Do you think I'll ever forget that?'' He suddenly grasped her upper arms in firm hands and shook her. ''The sight of your beautiful body knocked ten feet through the air before crashing against solid concrete? Or the blood in your hair when only an hour before it shimmered like gossamer? How about those stunning eyes closed to me, possibly forever? How about your luscious mouth blistered beyond recognition by heat so intense, a dozen men went to Emergency suffering exhaustion?'' His chest heaved. ''Do you honestly believe I'll be able to put that picture out of my mind?''

''Grady—'' Her voice came out on a gasp. She placed her palms against the warmth of his chest, too shocked by his emotional outpouring to think coherently. His heart galloped beneath her hand.

''Touch me,'' he begged, covering her hands with his own to slide them around his neck. ''Kiss me, Gina. I've needed to feel you like this for too long,'' he confessed, his voice ragged, breathless. Gina couldn't believe any of this was happening and lifted tremulous eyes to her ex-husband. The eyes staring back were hot coals of desire, blazing for her. ''If anything, I want you more now than when we were married.''

His dark head lowered, blotting out what little light there was in the bedroom. With a low moan, Gina surrendered her mouth to his, giving herself up wholly to the one man she loved—loved beyond comprehension. The hunger for him grew, even as it was being appeased. She felt that her bloodstream was full of shooting stars as he deepened their kiss, literally swallowing her alive. She had no idea how long they tried to devour each other.

Grady couldn't seem to get enough of her. His magic hands slid into her silky hair, cupping her head to give him easier access to her eyes and mouth.

Her lips chased after his, allowing him no respite as they both clung, delirious with wanting. Like water bursting over a dam, they were caught in a force beyond their control.

"I've dreamed of this so many times," she whispered feverishly, pressing hot kisses against his neck, drowning in the feel and scent of him.

He crushed her voluptuous warmth against him. "I never believed the reality could surpass the dreaming. I'm not going to lie to you, Gina. I want you. So much, it's agony."

"I know. I feel the pain clear to the palms of my hands. I've been in this condition longer than you can imagine."

He groaned at her admission and picked her up in his arms. "Can't you see you were made to be loved? Your skin and hair, everything about you was created to entice me! I can't function any longer without lying in your arms again. Only you can put out the fire that's burning within me, Gina. Help me," he cried out.

His voice shook with raw need. Gina was no more immune to his pleadings than she was to his caresses. How many nights for years had her body been racked with a longing that only his loving could assuage? She wrapped her arms tightly around his neck as he carried her the short distance to the bed, burying her face in his black hair, glorying in the right to be loving him like this again.

"Promise me you'll always stay this way, Gina. I couldn't bear to think of you maimed or disfigured for no good reason. You're so beautiful it hurts," he whispered against her mouth as he placed her gently on the bed and moved to join her. "I'll fix it with Captain Blaylock at station 6. It'll minimize the dangers tremendously. I couldn't do my job the way I'm supposed to if I constantly thought I had to worry about you."

A gentle finger traced the fine-boned oval of her face before his lips followed the same path. "This exquisite face, this body, was meant for *me*." On that note he covered her mouth with smothering force to begin his lovemaking in earnest.

At first Gina was too entrapped by her own needs to think coherently. It might have been an hour instead of three years since they'd last made love; it was as if they'd never been apart. But slowly the realization dawned that they were no longer married and that Grady was assuming she'd abide by his conditions. She needed clarification on one crucial issue before Grady became her whole world once again.

She caught his face in her hands, but when she saw the degree of entrancement that held him, she almost couldn't ask the question.

"What?" he murmured, reading her expression with uncanny perception, kissing her bottom lip with a tenderness that was almost her undoing.

She swallowed hard. "Let's agree to worry about each other on the job. But you weren't really serious about what station I should bid or your ability to perform your own job, were you?"

Instantly a stillness settled over Grady. She watched the glaze of desire diminish until it was no longer there. Suddenly he looked older again, harder. A shudder racked her body, because she'd been the one to extinguish the light.

"I'm deadly serious, Gina," he finally answered, but she knew that already. Slowly he removed her hands from his face and slid off the bed, rubbing the back of his neck in a distracted manner that revealed his turmoil.

She got to her knees. "We're not married anymore, Grady. I have to live the life I've made for myself. Isn't that what you told me when I tried to dictate yours?"

His face was ashen. "So now the shoe's on the other foot," he said in a haunted whisper.

"No. That isn't the way it has to be," she cried out in despair. "Haven't we learned anything from past mistakes? I found out how wrong it was to try to make you into something you're not. We fought day and night because of it. Now I'm begging for your understanding. Why is this so different?"

Grady's intelligent face was a study in pain. "It just is."

"So now I'm going to have to bear the burden of guilt because the work I do affects *your* performance?" Her tightly controlled voice cracked before she could finish the sentence.

"Your coming back to Salt Lake has knocked my world sideways, Gina!"

She buried her face in her hands, wondering how to reach him. "In other words I should have stayed in California."

"It was a hell I could have endured," he muttered bleakly. He moved over to the window to stare out at the mountains. "Now it wouldn't matter where you went. You'd be in the thick of the action. Your chances of ending up a casualty are only outnumbered by the chances of ending up a quadriplegic. Or enduring a series of skin grafts and marrow transplants—for starters."

In a daze, Gina slithered off the bed. "We could both be killed in a car accident on the way home today. I learned in therapy that this kind of thinking is a useless expenditure of energy."

"If you're hinting that I need to visit a shrink, then you're way off base."

His words affected her like a slap in the face. "I wouldn't presume to make a suggestion like that. Only a wife has that prerogative."

He spun around. "Meaning that since I'm no longer your husband, I have no right to demand anything of you!" he lashed out. "You're right, Gina. We're both free to pursue our lives and our careers without interference from the other. As long as you're not at my station and you're out of my sight, you're at liberty to skydive if you want to."

"As it happens, I don't." She tried to inject a note of levity into the conversation. "Look, Grady. You said you brought me here hoping the atmosphere was conducive to some real communication. Isn't it possible for us to coexist in the same city without turning everything into a shouting match? We're bound to run into each other occasionally. I don't want to cower every time I see you coming." Her hands lifted in a pleading gesture. "On the strength of the love we once had for each other, can't we pretend to be civil and rational about this?"

His hands tightened into fists and the blood drained from his face. "You just don't understand, do you, Gina? And there's no way I can explain. I wish—"

Gina's head lifted, as she waited for him to finish. When he turned away from her without saying anything, she spoke for him. "I used to say that word like a litany when you went back to fighting fires. In my heart, I'd repeat over and over—I wish we lived somewhere else... I wish we'd never come home from the Middle East... I wish I could send you off to fight fires every day with a kiss and a sack lunch... I wish I had your baby..."

Her last statement hovered in the air like a live wire, sending out sparks. A flash of pain came and went in his gray eyes so fast, Gina wasn't sure she'd seen it.

"We can thank providence that's one mistake we didn't make," he said in thick tones.

Gina couldn't take any more and hurried out of the room and down the narrow staircase. They'd trespassed on quicksand at the mention of a baby. She fought the tears but it was a losing battle. To fill this adorable cottage with Grady's children had been her greatest secret longing. She closed her eyes in pain. So many dreams gone.

Cleaning up the remains of their picnic gave her something to do. Grady came down the front porch steps as she folded the blanket. His face was devoid of animation. She couldn't remember who had said that nothing was deader than a marriage that had ended, but the thought sprang to Gina's mind as she gazed at her ex-husband's face. Every time she thought she was making a little progress with Grady, the gulf seemed to widen even more. Yet, ironically, they were more physically compatible than ever. But physical desire alone couldn't compensate for everything else that was wrong. It might bring gratification for periods of time, but in the long run, giving in to their longings would only destroy them both. And Gina knew that any kind of relationship with Grady other than marriage would never satisfy her.

Grady put the picnic things in the trunk while she climbed into the passenger seat. "As long as we've come this far, I'd like to drive past Bridal Veil Falls on our way home," he said equably once he was in front of the steering wheel. "Any objections, or are you in a hurry to get back?" He spoke as calmly and matter-of-factly as if the scene in the upstairs bedroom had never taken place.

She took her cue from him. "I'd like that. My air conditioner at the apartment isn't working that well. I don't want to go back until absolutely necessary."

Grady nodded and started the engine. "Here." He handed her the scarf that she'd somehow lost on the bed and forgotten about. She thanked him and put it on, along with a pair of sunglasses, hoping to detach herself. But nothing could erase the sexual tension radiating between them. A fire had been started in the bedroom and only one fire fighter could put it out, she thought with a glimmer of ironic amusement. Then she sighed. It had been bad enough to work beside him day after day, but since he'd touched her, since she'd experienced the ecstasy of being in his arms again, this was agony in a new dimension.

Beneath his cool, implacable exterior, she wondered if he was suffering one tenth of her frustrations. Worse, she feared that he might slake his longings with that brunette he'd brought to the ball. Gina couldn't stand the thought of someone else being the recipient of his lovemaking. Not now...

She rested her head on the back of the seat and closed her eyes. It took every bit of self-control she possessed not to slide over and wrap her arms around his shoulders. She needed his kiss so badly....

He turned on the radio and fiddled with the tuner until he located a station playing soft rock. She found it merely distracting until the Beach Boys started to sing "Kokomo." Grady flipped to another station before she could ask him, and that one motion betrayed that his nerves were as taut as hers after all.

When they arrived at the turnoff for Provo Canyon and the falls, he suddenly turned left toward Salt Lake. She started to say something, but he silenced her. "I've changed my mind. Is that okay with you?" he practically growled at her. Even if it hadn't been okay, she wouldn't have dared argue with him in this mood. The atmosphere was explosive.

They arrived at her apartment an hour later. She got out of his car the minute he pulled to a stop in the driveway. She couldn't tolerate being in his company another minute.

To her amazement he got out of the car and followed her to the door. "I might as well take a look at your air-conditioning unit before I go."

"Th-That's all right, Grady. I've told my landlord about it. He'll be over in the morning to fix it."

He stroked his chin where the beginnings of a beard had started to show. "So...I'll leave it to you then to call headquarters and start bidding another station."

She nodded. "Thank you for the picnic. It was delicious."

He scowled. "It was a disaster and we both know it. No more games, Gina."

Her chin lifted. "I was thanking you for the food and the beautiful drive." Her voice quivered slightly.

In a totally unexpected move, he pulled off her sunglasses and stared at her face for a long moment. She didn't understand and her expression must have reflected it. "I'm taking one last, hard look at you, Gina. It's possible that the next time we happen to see each other, your face and body might be changed beyond all recognition."

He thrust the sunglasses into her hand and strode off toward the car. She could still hear the screech of tires a block away as she entered the apartment and collapsed on the couch, her body shaken by deep, racking sobs. The tears weren't just for what they'd lost. She also wept for Grady, because he'd just discovered what it was like to be afraid for someone else. It was the most isolated, lonely, horrifying feeling in the world.

CHAPTER SIX

SUSAN REACHED across the table and stabbed the rest of Gina's burrito with her fork. "May I?" she asked after the fact, swallowing the last of their Mexican-food lunch.

"Be my guest." Gina chuckled and finished off her Coke. Normally she had a healthy appetite, but since her trip to Midway with Grady she'd been too upset to eat much of anything.

"I take it you're not thrilled about being assigned to station 6," Susan said gently. "I'm sorry things are so bad between you and Grady. But maybe it's better not to be around him all the time under the circumstances."

"At first I thought so, too. But it's been almost three weeks since I last saw him. We haven't even bumped into each other at a fire. I spend the majority of my time going on building inspections. Nothing ever goes on at number 6. Would you believe I'm actually hooked on *Days of Our Lives*?"

Susan burst into good-natured laughter, which was so contagious Gina finally joined in. "What other stations did you bid?"

"Two and three."

"There'll be an opening at one of them pretty soon," she offered supportively. "If you don't mind my changing the subject, let's talk about our trip to Las Vegas. I told Nancy you and I would be rooming together. She and Karen want to be together, which leaves Mavis as the odd woman out."

"She can room with us. We'll request a triple. I like Mavis. She's a born comedian."

"So do I. Then it's settled." Susan smoothed her brown bangs away from her eyes. "I can hardly wait for the weekend. I've got fifty dollars' worth of nickels to play on the slot machines."

Chuckling, Gina shook her head. "You fool! Don't you know it's all rigged?"

"I don't care. A slot machine is kind of like a mountain. You climb it because it's there."

Gina grinned. "You're right. Just make sure you stick to nickels. Frankly, I think Las Vegas is the last place they should hold the union convention. We're all underpaid as it is."

"Too true." Sue cocked her pert head to the side. "Don't you like Las Vegas?"

"I think it's awful. In fact, I avoid it whenever possible."

"But Grady might be there...."

Gina averted her eyes. "If he does show up, he'll stay away from me. You don't know Grady when he digs in his heels."

Susan was silent a moment, her expression pensive. "For what it's worth, hang in there, Gina. I watched the two of you dancing at the ball." Her warm brown eyes softened. "If a man ever looked at me like that I think I'd die. He may try to act indifferent, but believe me, he was giving off the vibes."

"The situation has deteriorated since the dance," she murmured. "If you don't mind, I'd rather not talk about him." She cleared her throat. "What's happened with Ron?"

"I have no idea. Since I found out he has a wife, I've bowed out of the picture. He keeps leaving messages and I keep not returning them," she said in a bleak tone of voice. She eyed Gina soulfully. "We're a real pair, you know that?"

A sigh escaped Gina's lips. "Why don't we go play some tennis and burn these calories off?"

"Good idea. Let's go."

The heat was too intense for them to play more than one game, so they opted to swim and succeeded in wearing themselves out to the point that Gina fell asleep as soon as her head touched the pillow later that night.

She had only one more shift to go before the trip. Mavis called her at the station and offered to drive everyone to Nevada in her van. Her husband and children would have to get along with the Volkswagen for two days. The arrangement suited Gina just fine. She was sick of her own company. With Mavis entertaining them along the way, the time would pass quickly. For at least the weekend, Gina resolved to ward off all thoughts of Grady.

Fire fighters from around the country poured in to the hotels within walking distance of the convention center. The union planned to deal with issues ranging from employee benefits to the latest safety features in turnout gear. This year a session had been added to address the challenges facing female fire fighters.

Since there were too many workshops for one person to attend, Nancy divided up their group so the entire convention was covered and asked them to take notes. They could exchange information afterward. However, all of them planned to attend the women's session.

Gina enjoyed that session the most. It gave her an opportunity to meet women from every part of the country. The one point that emerged loud and clear was that it would take another generation before women were accepted as an integral part of the system. The guest speaker—a feisty Puerto Rican from the Bronx—brought the house down with her closing remark. "The old guard will have to die off first," she said, "but we'll handle it in the meantime. Right?"

The crowd went crazy, but Gina noticed that a few of the men in attendance were clearly not pleased. The very issue the women had been discussing was brought home a dozen times throughout the day. Loud comments and snickers, rude asides, came from corners of the room at every session Gina attended. Only a small number of men were responsible, but they managed to cast a pall over the activities.

After being propositioned for the third time just walking from one session to the next, Gina had had it and decided to go up to the room to wait for the others.

A couple of men were loitering by the elevator. They threw her furtive glances, then smiled. Angry at this point, Gina needed a release for the adrenaline flowing through her system and dashed up the stairs to the tenth floor.

"Is it my imagination, or are we getting unduly harassed out there?" she burst out the minute she entered their suite.

"I figured something like this might happen," Mavis said. "In fact, my captain warned me about it."

Sue didn't look too happy, either. "Nancy just phoned and said the same thing was happening to her and Karen. It's a put-up job. She thinks we ought to just stay in our rooms for the rest of the night and have dinner delivered."

"I agree," Gina said, nodding. "There's no way I'm willing to face that again."

They heard a knock on the door, and Sue, who was closest, answered it. Gina recognized the man as one of the two down by the elevators. "Is this where the party is?" he asked in a distinctly Southern drawl.

"Not unless you're into karate!" Mavis yelled out as Sue slammed the door in his face.

"I'm calling security," Gina announced, but before she could pick up the receiver, the phone rang. Her eyes darted to Sue. "What do you think?"

Mavis made a face. "It could be my husband."

"I hope it is," Gina said angrily. "Ask him to report the problem."

Mavis nodded and gingerly picked up the receiver. She put the phone to her ear, then held it out in front of her for anyone who cared to listen before putting it back on the hook. "Well, ladies. Shades of the Salem witch hunt."

"It's disgusting," Gina muttered. She tried to call the front desk but the line was busy. After five minutes of unsuccessfully trying to reach someone, her anger started to turn into resignation. She looked at the others and saw the same expression on their faces.

"I'd like to leave Las Vegas. The sooner the better," Sue stated unequivocally. Gina tried the phone again, even as Sue spoke. It was still busy.

There was another knock at the door. By tacit agreement no one moved. Gina kept phoning. The knock grew more persistent. "Gina? Are you in there?" a male voice demanded anxiously.

Gina's eyes locked with Sue's as the receiver slipped out of her hand. "Grady." Her heart in her throat, she flew across the room and opened the door. By the greatest strength of will she kept herself from leaping into his arms.

His penetrating gaze swept over her in one all-encompassing motion. "Are you all right? The troublemakers have been rounded up and dealt with. I tried to get through to your room but the line was busy."

Gina swallowed hard. "I was trying to phone security."

If he noted her pallor, he didn't say anything.

"It's good to see you, Captain Simpson," Mavis greeted him with a broad smile. Sue's eyes communicated a private signal to Gina before she joined Mavis in saying hello to Grady. Her glance clearly said "I told you so."

Grady was at his most charming, dressed informally in a cream sport shirt and dark gray pants. "Ladies, I'm afraid that sort of element will always be present at a function like this. Don't let it put you off. The night's still young." His dazzling smile took Gina's breath.

"Good," Sue piped up. "I'm ready to go hit the slot machines. Come on, Mavis. You can help me lose all my gambling money."

"I'm real good at doing that. Show me the way." They were out of the room so fast Gina didn't have a chance to say anything. She couldn't. After three weeks' separation, it was heaven just to look at Grady.

A slow heat invaded her body as his eyes took in the raw silk dress she wore, its color the exact shade of her violet eyes. "Did anyone approach you, Gina?"

"Yes," she answered in a breathy voice.

His eyes narrowed perceptibly. "Could you identify him?"

"You mean all three?"

She heard him say something unintelligible under his breath. "The hotel security officers are holding them downstairs. If you're able to make a positive identification, you can lay formal charges against them."

She rubbed her temples. "Much as I hate the whole idea, I'll do it. No women in any line of work should have to put up with that."

"I agree. Word will spread and—let's hope—prevent this from happening again next year. A couple of other women are also willing to cooperate. Would you like me to go down with you?"

"Please." Her eyes implored him.

"Then why don't we get it over with right now?"

Gina nodded gratefully and went downstairs with Grady. The whole process took only a couple of minutes. There was strength in numbers, and the other women showed no hesitation in picking out the men responsible for casting a blight on the conference. One positive outcome of the incident manifested itself in the tremendous sense of bonding Gina felt with the other women, and men, determined to stamp out this kind of behavior.

"Do you have plans for the evening?" He'd accompanied her to the door of her suite. She almost fainted at the question. The last time they were together he'd walked away from her in anger.

"No. You know how I feel about Las Vegas. I'd rather go back to Salt Lake tonight. The only reason I came was because Nancy said it would be a good experience and she's been at this a lot longer than I have."

His dark brows quirked. "And was it a good experience, apart from the obvious?"

She gave him a full, unguarded smile. "Yes. It did my heart good to see so many female fire fighters all assembled. The speaker in our section said there are more than forty women assigned in New York City alone. That's impressive, and it makes me more certain than ever that there's room for everyone if we're given half a chance."

His lips quirked. "That was quite a speech. You almost convince me."

She inhaled a deep breath. "To quote you, I'd be a liar if I said anything else. I used to love teaching school, but nothing compares with that moment when the gong sounds and the adrenaline spurts through your veins. You don't know what you're going to find till you get there, but you know somebody needs help. Instead of standing idly by listening to the sirens go down the street, you're able to respond. Qualified to respond. No wonder you quit your job at the newspaper."

They looked into each other's eyes for a long, silent moment. She couldn't read his enigmatic expression. But it was his next statement that really shook her. "I have to get back to Salt Lake tonight. You're welcome to ride with me. I'm leaving now."

She couldn't believe he'd made such an offer, not when every time they were together ended in pain and bitterness. She knew what she *should* do, but where Grady was concerned, she was willing to undergo anything to be with him. Even if they fought every step of the way. Grady left a void in her life nothing or no one could fill.

"Just give me long enough to gather my things and write a note to the girls."

He nodded his head, though his solemn expression made her wonder if he regretted the offer already. "I'll go down for the car and meet you in the breezeway."

She put a hand on his arm. "Thank you, Grady, and I don't just mean for the lift home."

A distinct frown marred his handsome features. "I guess it would do no good at this stage to point out to you that a female fire fighter faces drawbacks a man never encounters."

"You mean you've never been propositioned?" she asked with a sparkle in her eyes, trying to keep the conversation light. Already he'd introduced a sensitive subject, and he seemed determined to press on it, like repeatedly probing a sore tooth with your tongue.

A smile broke out, dazzling her with its brilliance. "Touché," he murmured mysteriously, removing her hand.

Her eyes narrowed. "I seem to remember a certain black-eyed belly dancer in Istanbul lying in wait for you on several occasions."

"Were you jealous?" he quipped playfully.

"I hated her."

Grady burst out laughing, the deep, rich kind of laughter that took her back to those heavenly days when they'd first fallen in love. "Believe me, sweetheart, she hated you much more."

The endearment was a slip of the tongue but it had the power to rob her of breath. And it caused Grady to revert to his inscrutable self. "I'll meet you downstairs in ten minutes."

Her hands literally shook as she hurriedly packed and dashed off a note to Sue and Mavis. She left a twenty-dollar bill on top of the note to pay her share of the gas. With a large family, she knew Mavis didn't have extra money to squander. Although she couldn't hope to fool Sue, she indicated in the note that the incident had upset her and Captain Simpson was willing to drive her home because he had to leave early for business reasons, anyway.

Grady stood by the Audi and put her things in the trunk before helping her into the car. "We'll grab a hamburger on the way out of town."

Suddenly a hamburger sounded divine. If they took the time to go to dinner at a restaurant, they wouldn't get served for an hour. And she couldn't wait to get away from people.

The stark beauty of the desert held Gina entranced for a long time. They rode in companionable silence until they reached St. George, where Grady filled the tank with gas.

Traces of fatigue fanned out from his eyes. Gina handed him a Coke and bought one for herself while he paid the attendant. "Would you trust me to drive your car for a while? You look like you could use a nap."

After a moment of uncharacteristic hesitation, he finally shook his head. "We usually end up with a speeding ticket when you drive. I'm not in the mood to be pulled over tonight."

Gina had the grace to blush, and Grady, ever alert, noticed.

"How many tickets have you had since you came to Utah? The truth now."

"Only one." The day she'd gone to see him . . .

He finished off his Coke and threw the can in the wastebasket. "That's one too many."

On that succinct note they got back into the car and drove on. Ironically, it was Gina who fell asleep en route and awoke a while later to discover that Grady had pulled off the freeway onto a side road at the exit leading to her apartment building.

"What's the matter?" she whispered, still disoriented from sleep. She raised her head from the window, rubbing her stiff neck. "Is something wrong with the car?"

"No."

That one word delivered in a still-familiar husky timbre set her pulses racing and she woke up fully. "Are you too tired to drive any farther?" she asked in a quiet voice, unconsciously running her palm up and down her silk-clad thigh.

"No."

A strange tension filled the car and she was acutely aware of his whipcord-lean body inches from her own. The ache that never truly left her throbbed to life, and she didn't know where to look or what to say.

"I want to make love to you tonight, Gina."

A moan escaped her throat. "Here?" She almost choked getting the question out. Was she dreaming?

"If this weren't such a public place, I'd say yes. I brought you back to Salt Lake tonight for that very reason. I want to take you home with me. If your answer is no, then I'll drive you to your apartment."

She couldn't believe any of it. "Grady—" She turned her head to stare at him. "I—I don't understand."

He was half lounging against the door, with one hand resting on the steering wheel. It was dark inside the car and she could scarcely make out his features. "What could you possibly not understand?" he asked wryly. "It's a simple yes or no."

Her mouth had gone so dry she couldn't swallow. "Nothing's simple where our relationship is concerned."

"We don't have a relationship."

Her cheeks burned crimson. "Then there's a name for what you're asking," she whispered.

He stifled an epithet and sat up. "I asked you for an answer, not a cross-examination."

She folded her arms across her stomach. "The answer is no."

He started the engine immediately. "That's all I need to hear." He drove back onto the freeway, and within a minute they were pulling up the driveway of her building.

"Grady—" her voice shook with emotion "—I don't know you like this."

He left the motor running and stared straight ahead. "Surely you don't put me in the same category with the other men in your life?"

It was on the tip of her tongue to tell him there were no other men in her life, but she didn't want to give him that satisfaction. The fact that he expected her to sleep with him—because *he* suddenly wanted to—hurt her deeply. Maybe she'd have flung herself at him if he'd asked her that question in the beginning, but by now too much had happened and she wanted more than a night of passion with him. She wanted all his nights for the rest of their lives. "If you mean that having been married to me once gives you special privileges, then you're mistaken. If we were dating again, it might be different, but we're not. As you said, we haven't got a relationship."

She heard the mocking tone of his laughter. "So if I were to begin courting you again, you just might condescend to offer me the pleasure of your delectable body?"

"If you started dating me again, I'd know why. The answer would still be no."

"Can you actually conceive of my ever asking you for a date? Because if you can, your imagination is more creative than mine."

She grasped the door handle. "You offered me a ride home from Las Vegas, for which I'm thankful. Let's leave it at that. What you want can be had anytime, anywhere, with anyone."

She got out of the car, slammed the door and walked around to the trunk, then realized it needed a key to open. Grady suddenly appeared. The moonlight revealed that the sarcastic smile was gone from his face, replaced by an expressionless mask. He handed her the bag and shut the trunk.

"Just so we understand each other, Gina. Tonight I wanted that total communion of body and soul we always managed to achieve in bed together, despite our problems. I thought you wanted it, too. Forgive me if it sounded like I was insulting you. I'll never ask you again."

Quickly Gina turned her head away. If he'd said *that* to her in *those* words, she couldn't possibly have refused him. Just when she thought she understood him, he changed everything around, making her feel the guilty party. It should have thrilled her that Grady could admit he still craved the intense, passionate bond they'd shared. But that wasn't enough. They probably wouldn't be able to stop at one night. In the end she'd be his mistress. From wife to mistress. It defied logic!

"It isn't possible to achieve a total communion when so much else is wrong, Grady. We found that out while we were married. You're choosing to ignore that part."

His gaze slanted toward her in the remote manner she'd grown to fear during their marriage. "You've changed, Gina. I've been looking for some vestige of the woman I married, but she's not there."

Gina blinked. "You divorced that woman, Grady."

His deep sigh seemed to reverberate beneath her heated skin. "A paradox within a paradox," he muttered cryptically, then reached into his trouser pocket. "I had rather elaborate plans for returning these to you tonight, but under the circumstances I'll just give them back now."

Gina couldn't imagine what he was talking about until he took her hand and dropped her diamond earrings into the palm. The moonlight turned them into a thousand little prisms. The significance of what he said hit her so hard she stood there like a statue. Grady had wanted to recreate their wedding night. Had he been planning this since her accident, the night of the ball?

"Did you even know they were missing?" he asked in a dull voice.

She put them carefully in her purse. "I assumed they were still in my turnout coat."

His smile was one of self-mockery. "A fitting place for them."

She couldn't let Grady think she was that callous. "I decided my turnout coat was the best hiding place for something so valuable. For your information, I bought a new turnout coat to wear at station 6. My old one is hanging in my bedroom closet. I had no idea you'd removed the earrings at the hospital, and since I've had no occasion to wear them, I had no reason to be—" She stopped and took a deep breath. "Why am I bothering to explain? You think the worst, no matter what I say or do."

"Am I that bad, Gina?" The teasing gruffness of his tone startled her, but it also told her Grady was satisfied with her explanation. Those earrings were sacred to her—and perhaps to him.

"You're much worse, actually. I have trouble understanding how you inspire such fierce loyalty among your crew."

He rubbed his lower lip with the pad of his thumb. "Then you should be grateful to have Captain Blaylock giving you orders."

"What orders? Rescuing kittens from trees, or dispensing plastic leaf-bags?"

His smile was complacent. "Look on the bright side. You've still got all your body parts in all the right places."

Gina ran a nervous hand through her hair. "If I don't get transferred soon, I'll be going someplace else to look for work."

"Where?" He fired the question abruptly.

"I'm going to California for the Labor Day weekend. If there's an opening at my old station in San Francisco, I'll take it."

There was a slight pause. "What's the attraction, apart from the fact that your parents live there?"

"I've always loved to swim, as you know. My station covered the harbor, boat fires, oil rigs, that sort of thing. I got into quite a bit of underwater rescue work, which beats watching soap operas in the afternoon."

He drew himself up, and she could see his muscles tauten. "What's this about, Gina? A little moral blackmail so I'll find a place for you at station 1?"

"I thought you were beyond blackmail of any kind, Grady. This may come as a surprise, but working at station 1 is not my aim in life. I'm planning for my future and I've been checking out all the possibilities here and in Northern California. Since none of the busy stations have openings here, and since it doesn't look like there'll be any in the near or distant future—for political reasons or otherwise—I don't have any choice but to go back."

She expected Grady to hurl some retort, but he remained unexpectedly silent.

"To be honest, it's not as hard to make it as a female fire fighter in California," she went on. "There are more of us down there and we're more accepted. I'm afraid Salt Lake is man's last bastion. You're in your element, Grady Simpson."

"You've changed almost beyond recognition, Gina."

"Then I have you to thank. To think if I hadn't met you, I'd probably be—"

"Dead! Blown up by a terrorist bomb. The American school where you taught has been a target many times in the past few years. The fact that you didn't leave Beirut when the government was urging all Americans to go should have warned me that you have an unhealthy sense of adventure."

Gina was incredulous. "Do you mean to tell me that all the time I was worried about you getting killed behind enemy lines, you were worried about *me*?"

"I felt that anxiety in the pit of my stomach from the moment we met." His voice rang with the truth.

"I can't believe it. You never said anything. I never knew."

"I never intended you to know. A man doesn't like to admit that kind of fear, not even to himself. All I knew was that I wanted you for my wife and dreamed about you becoming the mother of my children. I couldn't get you out of the Middle East fast enough."

She drew closer. "If you hadn't met me, would you still be over there?"

"In all probability, I'd still be a war correspondent somewhere on the globe."

Gina was aghast. "Did you love it so much?"

"I only loved one thing more," he whispered.

"Grady." She shook her head in a daze. "Why didn't you tell me any of this? When you found out you couldn't tolerate that desk job, why didn't you say something? I'd have gone anywhere with you."

He absently rubbed the back of his neck. "I wanted us to have roots, Gina. A real home, not some hotel room for two weeks at a time with five minutes' notice to evacuate. Fire fighting gave me the adventure I craved, and a home base as well. The best part was that I had my wife to come home to after a twenty-four shift. She smelled like flowers, was beautiful beyond description and held me in her arms at night. I knew that when I was away from her, she wouldn't be kidnapped or blown up or shot." Or knocked unconscious by a runaway fire hose...

Gina sagged against the fender of the car, unable to take it all in. He'd given up so much for her, only to be alone now. "Grady—after our divorce, why didn't you go back to the newspaper?"

"That only appealed while I was a headstrong bachelor without responsibilities. When you work in a war zone, you live on the edge. For me, that time has passed, Gina. Now you couldn't lure me away from the department. When I came back to Salt Lake, I came home, literally."

There was too much to absorb. Gina needed some time to herself to sort everything through. Grady had just revealed a side of himself she hadn't known about. He was more vulnerable than she'd ever imagined. His fears were as real as hers had been. Their lives were like a jigsaw puzzle with a piece askew. And every time you tried to fit it back in place, another piece was moved out of position until you couldn't remember how to put it all back together again. "I wish you'd told me all this three years ago."

His mouth thinned. "All the talk in the world wouldn't have affected the outcome." The air hung heavy with his parting comment, made all the more devastating because it was the truth. "See you around, Gina."

She let herself in the front door, then fell limp against it. *See you around, Gina.* To hear that from him after all they'd shared and lived through. It wasn't fair. She should never have come back to Salt Lake. Doing that had only plunged them deeper into pain. It was best for her to go back to California. Right now she couldn't relate to the Gina who'd reported to Captain Simpson one beautiful summer morning full of bright hope and expectations....

CHAPTER SEVEN

"Ms LINDSAY. The phone's for you."

"Thanks, Captain." Gina took the receiver from Captain Blaylock, a man the same age as her father with the same loving disposition and warm, caring spirit. "This is Gina Lindsay."

"Gina—thank heaven I reached you before you went off duty. Remember Jay, that fire fighter from engine 7 I met in Las Vegas? He took me to breakfast?"

"Remember?" Gina said, laughing, "he's all you've talked about for the past two weeks!"

"Well," Sue drawled, "he finally swung a shift that gave him today off. He wants to spend the whole day with me. And if everything goes the way I hope it does, we'll end up at my place for dinner."

"That's wonderful." Gina was really thrilled for her.

"And he has a friend. Another fire fighter you once swung shift with, Stephen Panos. Remember him?"

"Yes. He could pass for a younger Omar Sharif."

"You noticed!"

"I noticed. He's nice."

"Well, he noticed you, but he's never been able to work up the courage to ask you out, because your blasted rules precede you."

"You know why I've had to stick to them, Sue. I haven't wanted to give Grady a reason not to trust me."

"Look, I don't mean to sound cruel, but does it really matter any more what he thinks? You haven't seen or heard from him since he drove you home from Las Vegas. You admitted to me that it's really, truly over this time. So break your rules and come out with us today. Please. How long has it been since you went out on a real date, Gina?"

"A date?" she repeated.

The captain smiled, forcing Gina to turn her back on him. She sighed. "A long time, since before I came back to Salt Lake."

"*That* long?" Susan gasped. "You're way past due, my friend. We're going to play a little tennis, swim, get acquainted. That's all. What do you say?"

"Well..."

"Do it," the captain barked without lifting his head from his stack of paperwork. "That's an order."

Gina laughed. "Sue? Did you hear? Captain Blaylock just ordered me to go with you. How about that?"

"Tell him he'll receive a medal for cooperation in the line of duty. Gina—do you mean it? You'll come?"

She took a deep breath. "Why not? I probably won't be working in Salt Lake much longer anyway."

The captain's head came up. "What's that?" He frowned. She really had his attention now and could have kicked herself for what she'd said.

"Nothing, Captain."

"I didn't like the sound of that. You and I need to have a talk before you go on vacation."

"Gina, the guys will be by for me in a few minutes, then we'll come for you. You can leave your car there, can't you?" Sue's voice dragged Gina back to their conversation.

"Sure. That's fine. But remember that I've been on duty twenty-four hours. And I look it."

"That's the beauty of keeping it in the family. We all look awful. Who cares? They appreciate us on the inside."

Gina started to chuckle. "Wouldn't it be nice if that were true?"

"It's going to make Stephen's day, Gina. You might even enjoy yourself. Thanks for being a good friend. See you in a little while." Gina mumbled her good-byes and hung up the phone with trepidation.

The captain looked at her for a full minute, waiting for an explanation. "It's obvious you're not happy here, so we need to discuss the problem," he finally said. "Go have fun today, but remember that you and I will have a talk." He sounded just like her father and was every bit as kind. Best of all, the captain was one man who didn't have a problem with female fire fighters. What a difference that feeling of acceptance made. "Thanks, Captain. I promise we will."

In the bathroom she changed into Jamaica shorts and a T-shirt. With a little effort, she soon felt halfway presentable. It seemed so strange to be getting ready for a date. She wondered if she'd ever overcome the pangs of guilt, the sense of being disloyal to Grady by going out with another man.

The new shift arrived as Gina was walking out the door to put her things in the car and lock up. They exchanged greetings and kidded around until Sue arrived in Jay's car. Stephen got out of the back and ambled slowly toward Gina.

"What do you know," he said, giving her a wide smile. "Everyone said it couldn't be done, but here you are in the flesh, Ms Lindsay. Unless Sue's putting me on, she says you're willing to spend an entire day with me. Is that true?"

Gina always thought of Stephen as the strong, silent type, but he had absolutely no trouble communicating and was even more attractive than she remembered. "Only if it's what you want, Mr. Panos."

He eyed her appreciatively. "I've been wanting a date with you since your first day on the rig. I'm not even going to ask why the fates have suddenly decided to deliver you into my hands."

"We can thank Sue, I believe." She smiled back.

"Oh, I do." He nodded his head slowly. "I don't know about you, but I have the feeling this could be the start of a memorable relationship. Shall we go?"

In some ways Stephen reminded her a little of Bob Corby. He was confident and at ease with women but didn't have Bob's arrogance. Gina liked that about Stephen and realized that if she weren't so deeply in love with Grady, Stephen could be a man she'd be interested in.

Sue introduced Jay to Gina, and plans were made to go to breakfast. Over waffles and sausage they mapped out their day, which they filled to the brim with tennis, swimming, videos and some napping in between activities—inevitable, since they'd all been up for twenty-four hours before that.

It was almost ten o'clock by the time they called an end to their relaxing, fun-filled day. Stephen borrowed Jay's car long enough to drive Gina back to the station for her own car. He seemed reluctant to let her go.

"I'm off duty the day after tomorrow. Will you spend it with me? My folks have a cabin on Bear Lake. We could water-ski."

Gina rubbed her eyes with the palms of her hands. "If I weren't going out of town, I'd love to."

"Where are you going? For how long?"

"I'm going to spend Labor Day with my folks in Carmel, then go on to San Francisco. I'll be gone about a week."

"A week, huh?" He frowned. "I guess I can last that long. Barely," he amended.

"You're very nice, Stephen. I've enjoyed this day a lot. I'll call you when I get back. All right?" She couldn't believe she was saying that to him. Maybe she was just using him because she was in so much pain over Grady. If that was true, then it wouldn't be fair to Stephen, but she wasn't in a position to have a perspective on her emotions right now. Stephen had been divorced for five years, and unlike her, didn't seem to have any obsessions about the past. At least, not outwardly.

"I wish this weren't our first date, Gina. I'd like to kiss you good-night." Stephen was always direct. In that respect, at least, he reminded her of Grady.

She flashed him a smile. "Didn't someone once say that getting there was half the fun?"

He had an attractive chuckle. "Whoever said it was right, but I can assure you I'm going to get there, Ms Lindsay."

"Is that a warning?"

"It's a promise." His black eyes sparkled.

He started to get out of the car but she put a detaining hand on his arm. "Don't bother. My car's right next to us. Good night."

"Good night," he said reluctantly, gently squeezing her arm. She got out of the car and shut the door, then threw him a cheerful wave. He tooted the horn a couple of times and drove away while she started to unlock her car.

"I thought he'd never leave," someone muttered behind her. Gina whirled around in stunned surprise.

"Grady?" she cried out as her heart began to thud unmercifully. "How long have you been standing there?"

In the moonlight, his eyes glittered silver. "Long enough to feel sorry for the poor devil. He could hardly keep his hands off you."

"It's not nice to spy on people." She said the first thing that came into her mind, too disturbed to think coherently.

"Your protracted good-night was done in plain view of anyone who happened to be in the parking lot. The fact that I've spent two hours here waiting for you has nothing to do with it."

"Two hours? What could be that important? I'm tired, Grady, and it's been a long day."

"I'll just bet it has," he bit out fiercely.

She opened her car door. "Why don't you say what's on your mind so I can go home?" All day she'd actually managed to subdue the inevitable thoughts of Grady and she'd had a pleasant time for once. Now, within seconds, he'd reduced her to a trembling mass of nerves and desires. "I'll follow you. What I've got to say is going to take awhile."

"No, Grady." She swung around, the light catching the purple sparks in her eyes. "We've said it all. Over and over again. I can't take it anymore."

"And you think I can?" he lashed out, sounding breathless. "You've got your choice. We can talk here where someone from the station is sure to see us, or we leave and go someplace private. Preferably the condo. It's a lot closer than your apartment."

In truth, the condo *was* closer. And she had her car; she could leave whenever she wanted. She couldn't imagine what he wanted to talk to her about, but judging by his anger, it wouldn't be pleasant. "I'll follow you," she agreed at last.

He couldn't be jealous of her date with Stephen. That would imply that he still cared for her, which he didn't. Maybe he intended to upbraid her for breaking her promise not to get involved with a fire fighter. The questions plagued her until she wanted to scream. But what terrified her most of all was this tremendous power Grady had over her. All he had to do was beckon and she came running. He was her obsession and the longer she allowed the situation to continue, the less chance she'd have of ever carving out a little happiness for herself. Her plan to win him back had blown up in her face, just as her mother had predicted.

In a few minutes she'd parked her car and was following him up the stairs as he took them two at a time to the living room of the condo. She unwillingly admired the fit of his Levi's. He had a magnificent body and he moved with fluid grace. Every motion, even the way he ate his food, intrigued her.

"Can I offer you a drink? Some wine?" Suddenly he'd turned into the urbane host and it confused her.

"No, thank you," she murmured, sitting down on the small love seat opposite the leather couch. "Please say what you have to say, Grady. I'm exhausted."

His eyes played over her suntanned face as he stood in front of her with his hands on his hips. "I can tell. Under the circumstances it might be better if we made you more comfortable." Lightning fast, he swooped down and picked her up in his arms. Her cry of surprise was smothered by the mouth that closed over hers, demanding a response. He carried her to the couch and sat down with Gina still in his arms, lying across his lap.

He hadn't given her time to think. She only knew that this was Grady holding her, kissing her as if he were trying to summon the very breath from her body. The terrible thing was that Gina gave him what he wanted, because it was what she wanted, too.

"Grady—love me. Please love me," she begged, burying her face in his black curls, curving her body against him. His strong legs wrapped around hers and ignited something deep inside that made her body go molten.

His hands entwined in the silk of her hair and he held her fast. That incredible translucence was there in his eyes. "I want to do much more than that, Gina," he said thickly. "I want to marry you."

Silence fell over the room, and the only sound Gina could hear was the pounding of her heart.

She traced the outline of his sensuous mouth with her finger, as if bewitched. Her eyes were twin fires of purple gazing up at him. "Do you have any idea how long I've been waiting to hear you say that? Grady—" She grasped his face between her hands and searched hungrily for his mouth, giving him her answer.

Suddenly Grady crushed her to him and buried his face in her neck, holding her so tight there was no space between them. "Sweetheart," he whispered with the old tenderness and the trace of tears in his voice. Gina was already in tears and they fell between her dark lashes, wetting them both.

"If I die tonight, it will be from too much happiness," she confessed.

"Don't die on me now." His body shuddered as his mouth found hers and feasted on it till Gina felt drugged with desire. "I have plans for us," he whispered at last, brushing his lips against her eyes and nose.

"So do I."

He caught her hand to his mouth and kissed the palm before putting it against his heart. "Can you feel that?" His mouth curved in that half smile that always sent her into shock with its male beauty. She nodded in a daze. "It beats for *you*, Gina."

A new radiance illuminated her face. "I came back here—to Salt Lake—for you, Grady. You're the most precious thing in my life."

"Thank God you did." His eyes blazed with a silver fire. "I was a fool to ever let you go." His voice shook with urgency and with a self-recrimination that wounded her.

Gina's eyes searched his. "We had a lot to work out, Grady. But we've found each other again. Our marriage will be much stronger than it was before."

His face sobered. "I came to California so many times you never knew about. I even watched you riding horseback along the beach one day, but I could never bring myself to let you know I was there."

"What?" Gina's heart leaped in her breast. "I thought you'd forgotten all about me. Never a phone call or a letter. I've never known such pain."

"Gina..." He buried his face in the silken profusion of her hair. "What have we done to each other? These past three years have been an eternity. I've been surviving, but you wouldn't call it living. I don't think I could describe how it felt to see you standing there at the desk. You were the most beautiful sight I ever saw in my life."

"Then you're the greatest actor alive, my love." His head lifted at that. "I was literally sick to my stomach, I was so frightened by what you'd say or do." Her eyes glistened. "I couldn't bear to think it was really over between us. I had to find out."

"I told you once how courageous you are. I'm in awe of it, Gina," he confessed, his voice softened by an unfamiliar humbleness. "I don't deserve a second chance, but because of you I've got it and I'm not going to do anything that will ever hurt you again. At least, not knowingly."

Gina stared long and hard at him. "I love you, Grady."

He swallowed visibly. "I love you. Will you accept the house in Midway as a belated wedding present? I bought it hoping that one day, by some miracle, you'd live in it with me. I never gave up on us, Gina. I just didn't know how to reach out to you. Every way I turned there was a stumbling block."

"Grady..." She played with the black tendrils curling over his bronzed forehead. "Let's not dwell on the past anymore. The time's too short. Can we have a baby right away? It's all I can think about since we drove to Midway."

"Why do you think I drove you there, if not to torture you with the idea? If you couldn't be the mother of my children, then I didn't want anyone else. But first—" he tousled her hair with his hand and kissed her mouth firmly "—I'm planning to fly down to California with you. I want to formally ask for your hand in marriage. I couldn't do that the first time around since we were out of the country."

She grasped one of his hands between hers. "Mother told me I was crazy to try and win you back. She couldn't see that going to Salt Lake would accomplish anything but more pain. It's going to be a shock for Mom and Dad when you come home with me."

"A good one, I hope."

"They love you, Grady. They'll be ecstatic. It's the fire fighting they hate."

"Somebody has to do it."

"I know." She laughed playfully. "But they're more resigned to the idea than they used to be."

"Would you like to be married in California?"

"No, my home is here with you," she said firmly. "I'd like to be married in a church, with all our friends from the various stations joining us."

Grady groaned. "I'm not sure any of my crew will be speaking to me when they find out you were really my ex-wife. I even have it in my heart to feel sorry for Corby—despite the fact that I could have strangled him with my bare hands the night of the ball. He can thank providence you stuck to your rules."

Gina looked sheepish. "Except for Stephen Panos."

His eyes glittered possessively. "How many times have you been out with him, Gina?"

"Today was the first."

His chest heaved as he played with a strand of her hair. "I figured as much. Otherwise he wouldn't have let you go so easily."

Stephen was going to be shocked when he heard the news. She'd given him no clue that anyone else was in the picture. "I'll have to tell him soon." She slanted a provocative glance at him. "What about that brunette? From what I saw, you're going to have a slightly harder time of it."

"Don't worry about that," he murmured against her mouth.

"It's worse than I thought," she shot back.

"I love it when you act jealous. But I'll tell you a secret. Among my many sins throughout our marriage, infidelity was never one."

Gina's heart raced. "And after the divorce?"

Grady tousled her silken hair. "After a time I dated my fair share of women, but compared to you, Gina, there's simply no contest." His eyes narrowed and he caught her face between his hands. "Has there been a man in your life?"

She gazed at him tenderly. "Yes. There was one."

He blinked and she saw a brief flash of pain in his eyes. "You don't have to tell me. I don't think I want to know."

"Darling." She lowered her mouth to his. "It was you. Some women can only love one man. It's the way I'm made."

Grady let out a long, sustained breath and the beautiful smile that broke out on his face made him look ten years younger. "Gina—" He began to shake his head, and suddenly she was crushed in his arms once more. "You've made me the happiest man alive." Gina clung to him for fear he was an illusion and might disappear at any moment. "Let's get married over the holiday. As soon as possible."

She nodded, rubbing her cheek lovingly against the slight rasp of his. "We can get our blood tests in the morning."

"Do you want to live here at the condo, or shall we find a place closer to Midway, so we can get there sooner on our days off?"

"We'll never find a better view of the valley than the one we have right here. Let's stay here for the time being. Maybe when our third baby is on the way we can look for a bigger place."

"It looks like I'm going to have to keep you busy in that bed if we're going to produce all those children," he whispered against her ear, biting the lobe gently.

"That's the part I'm looking forward to." Her voice was suddenly choked with tears. "I've missed you so terribly, Grady."

"I can't even talk about it," he admitted. "Let's go upstairs. I'll show you what it's been like for me."

Gina's answer was to nestle closer as he picked her up in his arms and started for the spiral staircase leading to the master bedroom. He paused on the way up to drink deeply from her mouth.

"Grady," she whispered, raising passion-glazed eyes to him. "Do you think you could throw some weight around at headquarters so that our schedules are the same? We're going to need all those days off together if we're going to have that big family."

His smile was mysterious. "Sweetheart, you don't need to keep up the pretense any longer. Tomorrow you'll hand in your resignation. You're going to be my wife again. That's all that's important." He continued on up the stairs and strode into the bedroom, carrying her over to the window so they could look at the view together.

"What pretense are you talking about?" She kissed the side of his neck. "What resignation?"

Grady gently lowered her until her feet touched the floor. He pressed her against him and put his hands on her shoulders. "Gina, you've proved to me that you've overcome your fears. You're the most amazing woman I've ever known. But there's only going to be one fire fighter in this family. I want you home, safe and sound, loving me and our children. I don't know another woman who would have gone to the lengths you did to fight for her marriage, but the fight is over, sweetheart. You've won. Thank God nothing serious ever happened to you before we found our way back to each other. Now, no more talk. I'm going to love you all night long. I need to love you." His voice shook with naked emotion.

The blood drained from Gina's face and she felt light-headed. When he started to draw her toward the bed she resisted. She felt as if a steel vise trapped her, constricting her breath. The plunge from heaven to hell was swift.

Grady's brow furrowed in concern and genuine surprise. "What is it? Your skin's gone so pale."

"Hold me, Grady," she cried out. "Hold me and listen."

He clutched her to him and for a few seconds, she rested in the strength of his arms. "What's wrong, Gina? Are you ill?" He sounded anxious.

"Yes. I'm ill." She tried to swallow. She didn't know how to say what needed to be said. "How do I tell you this without the pain starting all over again?"

He didn't have to say a word, but she felt some intangible energy leave his body. He didn't stop holding her, but the oneness had stopped flowing between them, leaving her bereft once more.

"I don't want to resign, Grady. I love my work. I— I thought you understood. I thought you'd come to terms with it. And all this time you thought it was a pretense." He started to pull away from her, but she held on to him fiercely and wouldn't let him go. "Listen. Please."

"No!" he cried out, shaking his head. Now his skin looked like parchment. "Don't tell me this now. I can't take it." She'd only seen tears in his eyes on one other occasion—the day he'd told her he couldn't go on, that he was divorcing her. With almost superhuman strength he broke free of her arms and took a step backward, as if he were dazed. "I *refuse* to believe you love the job enough to let it come between us, Gina. You *couldn't* love it. It's the most dangerous job in the world! It's dirty and hard and exhausting and often terrifying. It's no place for my wife!'' His face had a pinched look.

"Why isn't it?" Gina's chest heaved. "Am I exempt from the more unpleasant aspects of life?"

"Come off it, Gina. *The more unpleasant aspects of life,*" he yelled. "Have you ever seen the charred remains of a buddy when you couldn't get to him in time? *Have you?*" The tension that gripped him made the cords stand out in his neck. "Well, I *have!*" he answered without waiting for a response. "I've seen five men vaporize in a fireball and I couldn't do a damn thing about it. I'm still haunted by those memories. It could happen to you, any time, any day of the week."

"Of course there are risks, Grady. *You* take them every time you go on duty. But think of the good we do, the service. There's no other feeling like it. I hoped we could always be together, work together. I thought you'd changed and wanted that, too."

"Then you were wrong."

She closed her eyes in pain. "I love you, Grady. I'll always love you, but I guess this really is goodbye."

"Don't ever come near me again." Eyes of flint pierced through her as he delivered his ultimatum.

That moment would stand out in Gina's mind and heart as the blackest of her life. She never remembered her flight from the bedroom or her drive back to the apartment.

CHAPTER EIGHT

"CAPTAIN BLAYLOCK?" Gina poked her head into one of the offices at headquarters, gratified to find the captain alone. Sunglasses hid her puffy eyes.

"Good. You're here. Come on in, Gina. I know you're getting ready to go on vacation, but I thought we'd better have things out before you go away." Gina nodded and entered the room, finding a seat opposite the desk. She felt like death and hadn't slept all night. Like a person in shock, she'd sat on the couch staring into the darkness. Captain Blaylock's phone call was the only thing to rouse her from a near-catatonic state.

He sat back in the swivel chair and touched the tips of his fingers together, eyeing her curiously. "I raised five daughters," he started off without preamble, "which qualifies me to read between the lines. You're a fine fire fighter and getting better all the time. But you have a big problem in your personal life." Gina averted her head, not so much surprised by his frank speaking as by his astute observation. "Nothing you tell me will ever go beyond this room, but I want to know what's going on. In time, this problem will start to affect your job and then we're all in trouble. I heard you mention Grady Simpson's name on the phone. Let's start with him.''

Gina tried to find words but nothing would come out, and to her humiliation, giant tears rolled down her cheeks. She took off the glasses to brush them away. The captain sat forward.

"I've known Grady a long time and they don't come any better, but if I don't miss my guess, something's going on between the two of you.''

The captain saw too much, Gina mused broken-heartedly, but she still couldn't talk as she attempted to stifle the sobs.

"I checked with Captain Carrera this morning and he had no complaints about your work, profession-ally or otherwise, which leads me to believe the trouble started when you went to station 1. Are you in love with Simpson?''

Gina's gasp resounded in the room and the captain nodded. "I thought as much after watching the two of you at the Fire Fighters' Ball. My wife made the comment that she'd never seen two people who looked so much in love and I agreed with her.'' He paused. "Have you quarreled? Is that what this is all about? Because if it is, you need to straighten things out for both your sakes and the good of the department. Gina? You're a lot like my daughter Kathy. You're proud and you try to stay cool, but inside you're mush.'' Gina's strangled laugh broke the tension. "Forget I'm your superior and just talk to me as a friend.''

"You should have been a psychiatrist." She sniffed hard. "In order for you to understand, I'll have to tell everything and I'd hate to keep you that long when it's your day off."

"Why do you think I'm here?" He chuckled. "I'll be retiring in October and to be honest, I'm dreading it. I've been at this job forty-five years. It's all I know. There's nothing else I'd rather do than try to be of help."

Gina could tell he meant it. "You're one in a million, Captain."

He smiled kindly. "Well, if that's true then you know you have nothing to fear from me."

"I know," she said, nodding. "Well…it all started in Beirut," she began, as if that explained everything.

His eyes crinkled. "As in Lebanon?"

"Yes," she replied, running an unsteady hand through her hair. "That's where Grady and I first met and fell in love." Having said that, Gina felt as if the barriers had come down, and she bared her soul. Except for the intimate details of their life, the captain knew everything by the time she was through speaking. She'd even told him about her plan to look for work in California.

He stared at her for a long time, just as her father always did when he was mulling over an important decision. "What was it John Paul Jones said when all looked hopeless? *I have not yet begun to fight!*" Gina blinked in absolute amazement. "Where's your courage, my girl? Are you going to run away when the going gets rough? Where's the fighter who crawled around in all that smoke to rescue a two-hundred-pound man without batting an eye?"

Gina clasped her hands together. "You don't know Grady. His fears are much worse now than mine were in the beginning."

His brows lifted. "And then again, maybe they also hide something else. Have you thought of that?"

Their eyes met. "Like what, Captain?"

He shook his head. "I don't know. But maybe you ought to think about that while you're visiting your folks. Then come home and show what you're made of. No one knows what the future holds, Gina, but if you don't come back, you'll never find out."

The captain had given her a lot to think about. "I appreciate your advice. Your daughters are lucky. I wish all the men in the department were like you. You're not threatened by women."

His bark of laughter resounded in the room. "You didn't know me in the days Nancy Byington came to the department. I was her first captain out of school and we lasted exactly one shift together."

"What?" Gina cried out incredulously.

"That's right. I didn't believe in women doing men's work. We'd never had a female on the force before. I thought it was a big joke. But that was before my Betsy went into engineering and Kathy into medicine. They managed to turn their old dad's thinking around in a big hurry. Give Grady some time. You're young, both of you. Anything can happen. But if it doesn't—" he lifted a finger "—you'll have the satisfaction of knowing that you gave it all you had. That way, you can go on.''

Unable to stay seated any longer, Gina covered the distance in half a dozen quick steps to give him a hug. "You're wonderful, Captain."

"That's what I like to hear." He laughed jovially, patting her hands. "Now go on down to Carmel and have a good time."

"I will." She squeezed his shoulder in gratitude, then started for the door, feeling strangely at peace. She wouldn't have thought it possible when he summoned her that morning.

"And Gina?"

"Yes?" She whirled around in the open doorway.

"We may not see as much action at number 6 as you did at station 1, but in order to be the best fire fighter there is, you need to experience it all. You'll learn things with us that you need to know, things you won't learn anywhere else."

How did he get so wise? "I already have, sir. I don't know how you've put up with me. I'll see you next Tuesday morning."

A broad smile broke out on his face. "I knew you were a fighter!"

The idea that Grady's fear masked something else stayed in Gina's mind constantly all the time she was in California. The reunion with her parents shed no new light, even after a lot of discussion, but she returned to Salt Lake after four days of pampering, determined to stick things out for the time being, to see where it all led. Captain Blaylock was right about one thing. If she didn't give Grady more time, she would always have a question, and it could mar any future happiness, period! Grady expected her to remain in California. She wondered what his reaction would be when he found out she'd decided to return to station 6. He'd told her never to come near him again, but if they both happened to be fighting the same fire, he'd be forced to acknowledge her presence, if only to himself. Right now, this was her only hope of reaching Grady, and she clutched at it like a drowning man gasping for air. It could be one hour or six weeks before an alarm went off that brought the two of them together, but she was beginning to learn the value of patience—thanks to Captain Blaylock.

Station 6 was located in a residential area on the northwest side of Salt Lake. Most of the runs involved heart attack victims or incinerator fires, accidents that happened in and around the home. Gina ignored the dispatcher's voice when the first alarm went out signaling a fire in City Creek Canyon, about three miles away. But strong winds hitting the valley were hampering rescue efforts and more units were called out.

"Let's go," the captain shouted, and Gina jumped into her boots and turnout gear before boarding the rig with Ted and Marty. Captain Blaylock called the battalion chief for more instructions as they crested Capitol Hill, where they could see flames licking up the steep gully. A string of expensive condominiums on top were threatened, and a call had gone out to drop chemicals from the air.

Gina's gaze took in the engines and ladder trucks already assembled, knowing that Grady might be among them, and her heart started to knock in her breast. It was three weeks since her return from Carmel, and she ached for the sight of him.

"Ted? You heard the chief. Drive down to Second Avenue and we'll swing up A Street. Gina, you and Marty go in with the hose and keep that garage watered down till more units arrive."

"Right, Captain," Gina murmured along with the others. When they arrived on the scene moments later, the end condominium was in the greatest danger of going up in flames. Other units were attacking the fire in the gully below.

The captain pulled the plug—attached the hose to the hydrant—with the efficiency of long experience as Gina glanced around and caught sight of a boy of eleven or twelve, standing next to his parents and sobbing his heart out. At least she assumed they were his parents, judging by the way they all held on to each other.

"We'll try to save your place," Gina shouted, reaching for the hose. "Is your car in there?" she asked the father.

"Yes." His voice shook with emotion.

"Any gas cans?"

"One. But there's also my son's new puppy—he crawled under the car and won't come out."

Gina could remember her first puppy and she darted compassionate eyes at the boy. "What's his name?"

"Chester," he said on a half sob. "He's howling in there."

"We'll try to get him out. Ready, Marty?" she called over her shoulder. Marty gave the thumbs-up signal, and they began to pour water on the garage.

"Captain?" Gina asked as he approached to survey the situation. "We've got an animal in there, sir. I'd like permission to go in and get him. I can slide under the car more easily than anyone."

Captain Blaylock nodded his head. "I'll give you two minutes. That's it. If you haven't found the animal in that time, get out of there."

He took over her position on hose. Gina ran to the truck and put on her air mask, then hurried toward the garage.

Flames were licking around it and on the roof, but all Gina could see was the boy's heartbroken expression. She lifted the electric door manually. As soon as she did, she could hear the puppy's hysterical yelping and feel the intense buildup of heat. Gina groaned to herself when she considered inching her way under the gleaming red Porsche 911. Why didn't they own a Wagoneer instead?

She crouched on the cement and started calling to Chester. The puppy yelped a little harder when it heard her voice. "Come here, boy. Come on." She lay flat on her back and wriggled partially underneath the car. Her mask prevented her from going any farther, and she needed another couple of inches to grab the dog. Taking a deep breath, she removed her mask and glove and felt all around. Gratified when the dog's warm tongue started to lick at her fingers, she urged him on. "Come on. That's it," she crooned to him, and finally caught hold of an ear. He had to be a basset hound. She could hear the captain shouting to her.

"I don't like this any better than you do," she muttered, pulling the puppy out by the ear. He howled his head off, but she finally managed to get her arm around his wriggling body. He began to lick her face as she grabbed her mask and glove and dashed out of the garage, needing air before her lungs burst.

By now three hoses were trained on the garage and condo, containing the blaze. Gina's eyes searched out the boy, and she walked over to him, passing a group of other fire fighters.

"Chester!" The boy screamed with joy and hugged the puppy to him. His eyes were like stars as they looked up at Gina. "Thanks." That was all he said, but it was enough.

"You don't know how much this means...." The mother started to cry, leaning against her husband, who was talking to the captain.

"I think I do." Gina smiled as she watched the boy kissing his dog, murmuring baby talk to it.

"Our family dog died last month and we didn't think Max would ever get over it, but Jerry brought this puppy home the other night and it was love at first sight. If anything had happened to this one, I just don't know." She shook her head. "You've saved our house, too, and the car. We'll never be able to thank you enough. It's a good thing you're a woman," she added. "My husband was going to try and get down under the car, but he's too big and bulky."

"Did you hear that, Captain?" Gina winked, observing the cleanup operation out of the corner of her eye. But whatever the captain said in response faded away as her gaze connected with Grady's. He was standing patiently next to the boy, Max, listening to him and petting the puppy. *Where had he come from?*

"She's the one!" The boy pointed to Gina. "My dad couldn't get under the car, but *she* did." He ran over to her. "Do you want to hold Chester. He wants to thank you."

"I'd love to." Gina took the wriggling puppy in her arms, and he immediately proceeded to wet the front of her turnout coat. Gina started to laugh and couldn't stop.

Grady moved closer, his lips twitching. "It looks like you'll have to get your old turnout coat out of mothballs."

"Will you come to my school?" Max asked excitedly, unaware of any undercurrents. Gina tried hard to concentrate on the boy, which was almost impossible with Grady standing only a foot away. She couldn't have described the expression on his face, but he didn't resemble that other man who'd told her to leave and never come near him again. Her heart gave a kick. At least in front of his crew and the public, he'd decided to be civil to her and she could be thankful for that much positive reaction.

"You didn't answer his question," Grady prodded.

"Oh!" She looked away and tried to gather her wits. "You want me to come and give a talk?" She handed the dog back to him.

"Some of the kids get their parents to come if they have neat jobs. My mom works in a dumb office. I wish she rode a fire engine like you. Will you come?"

"Sure. Call station 6 and I'll see what can be arranged. I can do it on my day off."

"Cool!" A big grin spread on his face. "Hey, Mom! Dad!" He ran off to tell them, leaving Gina alone with Grady for a moment. There was activity all around them, but for some reason, Grady didn't seem to be in any hurry to get back to his crew. She should have been helping Marty with the hoses but she couldn't move. Again that tension streamed between the two of them, holding her fast.

"What are you doing back in Salt Lake, Gina? Wasn't there an opening in California?" Now that no one was around, the polite veneer had disappeared.

She tipped back her helmet so she could look at him squarely. "Captain Blaylock pointed out to me that I could learn a lot from working at station 6, so I didn't go to San Francisco. I'm going to stay in Salt Lake."

He cursed beneath his breath, but for one brief moment a haunted look lurked in his eyes before he recovered from the shock. "I hope you don't mean permanently."

"As permanent as one can be about anything, barring unforeseen circumstances." She stood her ground.

"I thought station 6 was too tame for you." He sounded angry.

"I was wrong."

His face darkened and his voice was dangerously quiet now. "What are you playing at, Gina?"

"Rescuing puppies from burning garages."

Another epithet escaped. "And underneath a car with a full tank of gas just ready to explode!"

"You know that's not true, Grady. That tank wasn't close to igniting. The—"

He cut her off rudely. "You know where you should be, don't you? You should be that woman standing there with a son of your own, dammit!"

She started to shake. "It would help if there were a *man* standing next to me, first!"

"I don't believe what I'm hearing." His hands tightened into fists.

"Believe it."

"We're ready to roll," Marty called to her.

"Tell him to go to blazes," Grady muttered. "I'm not through talking to you."

"I shouldn't have to remind you of all people that I'm still on duty, Captain." She'd never seen him lose control in front of anyone before, and the fact that he had was exhilarating to Gina.

"I'm warning you, Gina. Just stay out of my way."

Her chin lifted. "I'm trying to, but you won't let me, Captain, sir."

His eyes had gone black with anger. "So help me, Gina—"

She didn't stay to hear the rest. Everyone was on the rig waiting. Captain Blaylock eyed her flushed cheeks with interest as she climbed on board, and he gave her his secret smile. Nothing escaped the captain's notice. But if he thought Gina had some progress to report about her situation with Grady, he was mistaken. Grady was furious about her decision to stay in Salt Lake. Beyond that, she couldn't read his mind or his heart.

There was a message from Stephen Panos on her answering machine when she got home the next morning. She'd been putting him off since she came back from vacation. Although she liked him, she knew she could never feel more than that, and she had no desire to hurt him. Yet if she continued to put him off, she could easily end up living her life alone, something her parents harped on over and over again.

She finally called him back around three and he asked her to double with Sue and Jay for the fire fighters' annual Lagoon celebration. Besides the Lagoon Amusement Park attractions, there were going to be games and competitions among the crews, with a big barbecue in the evening and a dance to follow. She decided to accept the invitation. It wasn't an intimate dinner, after all. If she could keep things friendly and light, Stephen wouldn't be able to read any more into the relationship than was there. And if her real underlying motive for going with Stephen was to make Grady jealous, then she wasn't admitting to it.

Gina loved Indian summer in Salt Lake; September was her favorite month of the year. The days were hot and the nights cool. She dressed in a navy-and-white sailor top and white shorts for the outing and caught her hair into two ponytails. Stephen said teasingly that she looked sixteen, but the male appreciation in his eyes told her he wasn't complaining.

Sue and Jay had already fallen in love and seemed oblivious to most of what went on around them. Gina watched them with envy. Their relationship appeared uncomplicated and secure. Jay had no hang-ups about Sue's work. Again Gina was reminded of Captain Blaylock's statement that something else could be behind Grady's fears, but her frustration grew because she had no contact with him. She'd seen him twice since the episode with the puppy—once at headquarters when they passed each other in the hallway, and then at the downtown mall while she was doing some shopping. He walked by her both times without acknowledging her presence. That had never happened before, not even when they were both at their angriest during the divorce.

As each day drew to a close, Gina felt less and less confident that there could ever be a future with Grady. Maybe she was a fool to keep on hoping and longing for a sign, she thought. Then, at Lagoon, she saw him feeding cotton candy to the same brunette he'd taken to the dance, and she felt another bit of hope die out. Gina and Stephen had strolled along the path toward the picnic area where the competitions were being held, when she spotted Grady's curly black head among the crowd. In white aviator pants and shirt, contrasting with his bronzed skin, he made every other man around him pale into insignificance.

This time Gina paused to satisfy her curiosity about the woman who held his attention. She was Grady's age, sophisticated and attractive in a dark, almost Spanish way. Gina felt something snap inside her as the woman stood on tiptoe and kissed Grady's mouth after giving him back some cotton candy. In excruciating pain, Gina looked away but not quickly enough. Grady's startling gray eyes penetrated hers for an instant, their look triumphant.

Embarrassed to have been caught staring so openly, Gina turned to Stephen and suggested they sign up for the three-legged race. Jealousy tore at her insides; Grady knew how to get to her. The outing had lost its appeal and Gina wanted to go home. But because she couldn't, she assumed an artificial gaiety, trying desperately to put Grady out of her mind for the rest of the afternoon and evening. She encouraged Stephen to enter all the events with her. Two hours later, they were exhausted.

"How about a swim before the barbecue?" Stephen suggested. "Let's just lie back in the cool water and relax. How does that sound?"

"Heavenly."

"Good. I'm a little tired of crowds and I'd like to get you all to myself, even if it means underwater."

Gina chuckled nervously, recognizing certain signs. Apparently Grady had no difficulty enjoying a physical relationship with a woman even if his heart wasn't involved, but Gina couldn't give physical affection without love.

Under her clothes she wore a one-piece white bathing suit, so it took only seconds to remove her shorts and top and dive into the deep end of the Olympic-size pool. Stephen wasn't far behind. There weren't very many people in the water at this hour. Most of the guests had started eating over at the picnic tables.

They swam for a while, then Stephen grabbed hold of Gina's ankles and forced her to tread water. "I've got a terrific idea. Why don't I go get us a couple of plates of food and bring them back here? We can dance by the side of the pool and avoid the crush."

Gina had second thoughts but didn't express them. She took advantage of the time he was gone to get dressed in her top and shorts. Stephen looked slightly surprised when he returned with the food, but Gina barely registered his reaction because Grady was directly behind him, with the dark-haired woman clutching his arm. Apparently Grady had also decided to escape the crowds—at least that was what she thought at first, until he found a poolside table close enough to her and Stephen to be able to hear them talking. Gina suspected that Grady had intentionally set out to ruin her evening. He didn't want Gina, but he didn't want her paying attention to anyone else, either. Still, the niggling thought that maybe he was worried about her interest in Stephen gave her a whole new set of possibilities to consider.

He'd told her to stay away from him, yet he seemed to go to great lengths to make his presence known whenever they were in the same place together. Was he trying to force her out of his life by flaunting the other woman? Grady knew how deeply Gina loved him, and his amorous attentions to his date seemed calculated to make Gina miserable.

After a few minutes of trying to ignore Grady, Gina couldn't take any more and suggested to Stephen that they head back to Salt Lake. He readily agreed, probably because he hadn't managed to spend any time alone with her, after all.

"Stephen," she began as he pulled into her driveway, "I haven't been the greatest company in the world today. I could make up a million reasons, but the truth is, I'm still in love with someone else and until I can do something about it one way or the other, it isn't fair to go on seeing you. You're too nice, and I like you too much."

Stephen tapped the steering wheel with the heel of one hand. "I figured as much. Who's the lucky man?"

"It doesn't really matter, does it?"

"It might. Don't be angry if I wormed something out of Sue, Gina. She told me you'd once been married. If you're still in mourning, I'll wait until that period has passed. There's a difference between being in love and grieving, you know. I can speak with some authority on the subject."

"I know, Sue told me," Gina answered gently. "I'll be honest with you. I've never stopped loving my husband and I'm hoping that one day we'll get back together. It may not be possible, but I refuse to give up."

Stephen fastened his dark eyes on her. "Have you let him know you want him back? Does he realize you haven't given up?"

His questions surprised her. "We still have something to resolve. It may be insurmountable."

Stephen nodded and then got out of the car, coming around to her side to accompany her to the apartment. "You know where to find me if you ever decide things won't work out with him. I'm not going anywhere." He kissed her forehead and walked away.

Why couldn't she fall in love with someone as nice and uncomplicated as Stephen? Gina asked herself. Someone mellow and steady. Maybe she was crazy to go on loving Grady when nothing could come of it.

Her nerves were wearing thin, yet she had no one to blame but herself. Grady would marry her in an instant if she'd give up fire fighting, but what would she do with those empty hours while he was out on the job? Teaching school could never hold her now. If they had a baby, naturally she'd stay home with the child as long as possible and then resume part-time work with the department, but what if they didn't have a baby right away? During their five months of marriage she hadn't become pregnant. She and Grady would be right back where they started, but this time he'd be leaving her at home to go and do the work they both loved.

Gina knew herself too well. The boredom and the sense of loss would cause a fissure that would grow into another break, perhaps more devastating the second time around. To remarry only to separate again—she couldn't tolerate that. If she could just make Grady understand.

As she started getting ready for bed, an idea came to her. It was the only potential solution she could think of, thanks to what Stephen had said in passing about letting Grady know she wanted a reconciliation.

After a long debate with herself, Gina summoned the courage to phone Grady. Maybe he wasn't home, or maybe his girlfriend was there with him. Gina didn't know, but she had to talk to him while she still felt brave enough. He'd warned her to stay away, but a phone call maintained a distance between them. He could hang up on her, but something stronger than fear of rejection compelled her to try to reach him.

He answered on the fifth ring and sounded as if she'd wakened him from sleep. "Grady?"

The silence lasted so long, she thought he'd simply put the receiver on the side table and left it there so he could go back to sleep without fear of being disturbed by her again.

"What is it, Gina?" he finally asked in a flat voice.

"A—are you alone?"

He cursed violently and she quailed at his anger. "That's none of your business."

Her hand gripped the cord tightly. "I only meant that I wanted to talk to you for a little while, and if this is a bad time, I'll try to call you later."

"I'm on duty in six hours. Since no time is a good time for whatever it is you want, say what you have to say and get it over with!"

"I shouldn't have called. You're obviously not in any frame of mind to listen."

"Don't you dare hang up now!" he warned. "Let's get this over with once and for all. You have my undivided attention. What is it?"

She gulped, wondering where she'd found the temerity to approach him in the first place. "Grady— I've been thinking about us since the other night."

"There is no 'us,' Gina," he said on such a bitter note she could have wept.

"Maybe there could be if you'd just listen for a minute."

A small silence ensued. "When you hand in your resignation to the fire department, then we'll talk. Not before."

"What if I make a permanent home at station 6? What if I don't bid any other stations or do any swing shifts to busier stations? Could you live with that?" she asked with her heart in her throat. It was a compromise, but one that would allow her to do the work she loved and live with the man she loved.

"No, Gina. So don't ask."

His flat-out refusal to consider any options made her indignant. "But why? I thought it was the amount of action and the danger you objected to. If I'm willing to work at the quietest station in the city, why can't you accept that?"

"Because I want you home. Period."

Gina frowned. There was a world of emotion in his voice. She felt she was getting closer to the real problem. Her intuition told her something wasn't right here. On a sudden burst of inspiration, she asked, "Grady...does this have something to do with the fact that your mother wasn't home for you as a child?"

"Don't start psychoanalyzing me. Goodbye, Gina." With a simple click of the phone, their conversation was terminated. Gina sat on the bed in a daze. Her thoughts were flying.

Grady's parents had worked at the Salt Lake *Tribune* when he was a boy. But later on there had been a divorce, and his mother had gone to live on the East Coast, where she remarried. She still lived there, and as far as Gina knew, Grady had little to do with her. As for Grady's father, he'd remained with the newspaper until he died of a heart attack. Gina had never met either one of them.

Though Grady had told her everything about his life as a war correspondent, he'd been reticent about telling her the details of his family life. She knew it caused him pain, so she never pried.

Haunted by the little bit she knew, Gina tried to imagine what it would be like to have both parents working all the time, at emotionally draining, all-consuming jobs. Then, during the sensitive adolescent years, to have to deal with a divorce... Apparently he'd chosen to stay with his father when his mother left.

Was Grady afraid their children would suffer if Gina was a working mother?

Captain Blaylock suggested there might be something behind Grady's irrational fear of Gina's getting injured. She was beginning to think he was right. Grady didn't care that she'd been willing to compromise and stay on at station 6. To quote Grady, *he wanted her home. Period.*

Another thought occurred to her as she recalled how jealous and excluded she had felt when Grady spent so much time with the fire fighters. In those early days, she'd hated that other family. Was it possible that Grady felt excluded now that Gina had another life at the station?

She tried to think back to when they first got married. Had resigning from the school where she'd been teaching been her own idea or Grady's? Their whirlwind courtship had blotted out all other considerations, but she was quite sure Grady had asked her to quit so she would be free to travel with him. It made sense at the time; otherwise they couldn't have been together every possible minute. Besides, Grady had admitted his fear of her being injured if she stayed in Beirut.

Her mind spinning with unanswered questions, Gina flopped on her stomach and stared into the darkness. Somehow, some way, she had to force Grady to open up. Only he held the key to the riddle. Until she got to the bottom of this, there would never be a future with Grady. Never.

CHAPTER NINE

A WEEK WENT BY but Gina didn't see or hear from Grady. She was almost out of her mind with pain and made up projects to do at the station when they weren't out on calls. On one of her days off she made an appearance at the grade school attended by Max, the boy who owned the puppy Gina had rescued. Usually, she enjoyed visits with schoolchildren; they forced her to put aside her anxieties for a while. But watching these lively, carefree boys and girls only seemed to deepen her longing for a child of her own, and she returned to the apartment even more depressed than she'd been before. The phone was ringing as she walked through the front door, and she could hear Captain Blaylock's voice on the machine, asking her to call station 6 as soon as possible.

This was their day off, so she knew it had to be important for him to be at work. She dialed his number immediately. He didn't waste time talking but simply asked if she was free to help with an emergency. She rejoiced at the opportunity—anything to keep busy so she wouldn't think about Grady.

"Captain?" Gina entered the station in her coveralls and hurried right into his office. He was conferring with the captain of the other shift. They both looked up when she walked in.

"Sit down, Gina. Captain Michaels and I called you because we need your expertise. There's been a bad accident involving a truck and car—they've both gone into the Jordan River. We don't know any details but people are trapped underwater. A call has gone out requesting scuba divers."

"I'm on my way, Captain."

"Good. I'm coming with you." They all boarded the engine and headed west toward the river. "A rescue unit with special scuba gear is headed for the scene of the accident right now," Captain Blaylock explained.

It was a fairly warm September afternoon. At least, the weather was cooperating, Gina thought. Rescues at night required lighting and everything became even more complicated and difficult.

The crew listened to the battalion chief's directives as they roared down the driveway. Police had already cordoned off the accident site. Approaching the area where the vehicles had gone over the edge into the water, they could see the truck's skid marks. A little farther on, Gina saw the big semi lying in the river, three-fourths of it submerged on the driver's side. The other car was about ten yards downstream and totally submerged. The river wasn't swift, but if the people had been knocked unconscious at impact, the danger of drowning was just as great.

She saw a ladder truck farther down the road and knew it was Grady's. Station 1 would have been the first to respond. Heart pounding, Gina jumped down from the rig and ran the hundred yards to the rescue unit, where she would change into a wet suit and tanks. Gina had learned to scuba dive when she was a girl in California. It was second nature to her, and never had she been more thankful for those hours of training than now, when so many lives were at stake.

The battalion chief was waiting for her as she approached the jump-off point. "There were no witnesses when the accident happened so we don't know how many people are down there. Captain Simpson's already in the water with one of his crew, but they need help."

Gina nodded and did a somersault over the edge, carrying an extra set of tanks. Once she had her bearings, she gave a kick and headed for the truck, swimming around to the front where she could see Bob Corby extricating the driver without any problem. He was already giving the man air from his tank and motioned for her to go help Grady farther downstream. She nodded and shoved off once more, employing her strongest kick to cover the distance as quickly as possible.

The car was jammed against some boulders. It was a white Buick four-door, and as far as she could tell, the windows were closed. If the driver had been running the air-conditioning, there could still be enough air inside the car to keep the person—or persons—alive.

As she rounded the side she saw Grady using an underwater torch to get the door open. In the driver's seat was a young man and strapped next to him in a car seat, a baby. They appeared to be dead, but Gina knew you couldn't be sure until you took vital signs.

Grady was too intent on his work to realize who she was. When he could see that help had arrived, he pointed to the door and she immediately rested her tanks on a boulder and started to pull on the handle, lodging her right foot against the body for leverage.

At first the door wouldn't budge, but after a few more pulls it gave way. Grady went in first and unfastened the young man's seat belt while Gina grabbed the extra tank. She put the mouthpiece into the man's mouth as Grady pulled him out. As soon as the opening was clear, Gina dived into the car and put her mouthpiece into the baby's mouth while she unstrapped the car seat.

Then, tucking the baby under her left arm, she carefully backed out the same way she'd come in and started swimming toward the surface with her precious bundle. It had taken longer than she'd expected to go through the maneuver. Her lungs were screaming for air by the time she surfaced.

An ambulance attendant stood ready to take the baby from her, and Captain Blaylock put out his hands for her to grasp as she climbed up the riverbank and collapsed on the dirt for a minute, drinking in fresh air. When she felt recovered, she put on the mask and mouthpiece and dived once more to recover the torch equipment and check for more victims. There could have been another child or even an adult on the floor of the back seat. The impact of a car accident could sometimes cause amazing situations.

Gina entered the interior of the car, but to her relief there were no more bodies or any sign of a pet. As she backed out, she felt a hand on her thigh. Grady had come back, presumably to get the equipment he'd brought down with him.

As she maneuvered her way around, their eyes met. He motioned at the dashboard of the car and pointed to the keys. Since they were nearest her, she pulled them out of the ignition. Grady took them from her and swam to the rear of the car. Gina followed and helped him to raise the lid once he'd inserted the key in the lock. All they found were a couple of suitcases and a camera, to her relief.

Grady pulled everything out of the trunk while Gina reached for the torch equipment, and then together they kicked toward the surface. Gina felt a rapport so strong and binding with Grady that she didn't want to leave the water. This was the first time they'd actually worked side by side as a team. It was an exhilarating experience, something she'd been waiting for since she began her training.

"Nice work," the battalion commander saluted as Gina was helped from the water, Grady not far behind.

"Did anyone survive?" Gina asked as she whipped off her mask and removed her scuba gear.

"All three are breathing on their own, Ms Lindsay. I understand you were called in for this rescue on your day off. I'm recommending you for a medal. Your second with the Salt Lake Fire Department. We're happy to have you with us."

"Thank you," Gina beamed, shaking his hand.

"Grady..." he extended his hand "...you and Bob Corby did excellent work, too. Congratulations. The three of you did the cleanest, fastest work I've ever seen in a situation like this. I'm recommending medals for you."

Gina looked over her shoulder to see Grady's reaction. To her shock, he only nodded at the battalion chief and spared her a brief, impersonal glance before walking away toward the truck.

The blood drained from her face at his abrupt departure. Here she'd been feeling this incredible harmony and oneness with him, had hardly been able to restrain herself from throwing her arms around him and shouting for joy because they'd saved lives together. And all Grady felt like doing was walking away.

A pain too deep for tears weighed her down as she walked over to the rescue unit and changed back into her coveralls. Cleanup procedures were starting, and a tow truck had arrived by the time the engine pulled away from the scene and headed back to the station.

"That was beautiful, Gina," Captain Blaylock said, patting her hand. The others joined in with complimentary remarks. "I'm proud of you. That young father and his baby were on their way home from the airport for a reunion with his wife. Now it can be a happy one. This is what it's all about, eh, Gina?"

She couldn't speak, so she patted his arm instead. Right now she was fighting tears for herself, for Grady, for the plunge from happiness to despair. If Grady couldn't respond after a moment like this, she felt as if she'd come to the end of a very long journey.

It was dusk before Gina left station 6, but instead of going home, she turned toward the mountains. She needed to get away and really think. This was her long weekend off and it didn't matter how long she was gone or if she even told anybody where she went.

When she reached Heber City, she pulled into the Wagon Wheel Café for dinner. No one served better veal cutlets than the Wagon Wheel. The rescue had depleted her energies, and she ate everything she was served, including a piece of homemade rhubarb pie.

Full at last, Gina checked in at her favorite motel down the street, then took a walk through the center of town, savoring the crisp mountain air.

She'd come to a crossroads in her life. She could not go on working in Salt Lake. This had been Grady's territory first. She was the intruder, and Grady couldn't have made it more apparent. Even if he cared, which she seriously doubted now, he was deeply disturbed by something that he couldn't share with her, couldn't talk about. That left Gina no choice but to walk out of his life for good.

At a little past ten Gina went back to the motel to go to bed. Only a few miles away sat the little gingerbread house. For all she knew, Grady was there now. All she had to do was get into her car and drive there to find out. But it would profit her nothing and might result in an even more devastating conflict.

She tossed and turned most of the night, then sat at the table of her room and wrote out her resignation on the motel stationery. She had an obligation to give the department two weeks' notice. At nine, she left for Salt Lake.

After going to headquarters to leave her resignation for Captain Blaylock, she stopped by Sue's place but her friend wasn't home. Despondent, Gina went back to her apartment and put in a call to the movers to make arrangements for her return to California in two weeks. She requested some boxes, which were dropped off the next day so she could begin the arduous task of packing. Sue called her that night and they went out to dinner. Gina's friend was disappointed when she heard the news, but thought it the wisest course of action. At least that way, Gina could get on with her life. Gina promised to come back at Thanksgiving for Sue and Jay's wedding.

"I received your resignation, Gina," the captain said as soon as Gina reported for duty on the following Tuesday. "I'm sorry things didn't work out for you and Grady."

"Me, too." She heaved a sigh. "But he refuses to talk about what's really wrong. I've tried everything."

"Not everything, Gina. You could do what he wants and quit fire fighting if he means that much to you."

"I know. But without knowing *why* he wants me to quit working altogether, I'm as much in the dark as ever. Captain, you're right about Grady. There's more bothering him than just my job. I think it has to do with family problems, something that happened in his past, but he's never been able to open up to me about it. Without total honesty, we can't have a future together.''

"You're right. So it appears I'm going to lose one of the best fire fighters I've ever had at station 6. But until that time comes, there's work to be done. Because it's such nice weather this morning, several of the stations have decided to go do practice drills out by the airport. Let's check out the rig and go on over.''

Practice drills were killers, especially when you were wearing full turnout gear. Gina immediately spotted Mavis plugging a hydrant.

"Let's show these guys how it's done," Mavis whispered as Gina unrolled hose alongside her.

"Why not?" Gina chuckled. Mavis was like a breath of fresh air right now. A little friendly competition with the men would help keep her mind off Grady. But in that regard she was mistaken. The next time she looked up, there was Grady talking to some of the drill instructors. Apparently his crew had decided to join in.

"Hey, Gina!" The guys from station 1 all waved and shouted to her. She watched them take their place in the lines and had to admit Grady's bunch was an impressive group. She waved back and kept on working with Mavis. A little later the drill instructor announced that everyone would have to climb a ladder to the third-story window of the vacant building and bring down a live victim in a fireman's lift. *"A live victim?"* Gina muttered to Mavis in shock.

Mavis had the light of battle in her hazel eyes. "I guess they're trying to show us up, Gina girl. They'll be sorry!"

These were timed drills and every move and procedure was noted and marked. Mavis winked at Gina and off they went. Gina positioned her hands and feet as she'd learned in countless practice sessions, then started up the ladder. On the other drills, she'd beaten almost everyone's time; she wanted to come out first in this one, too. Maybe it was because Grady was here that she felt this sudden excess energy. Whatever the reason, she scurried up the steps as if her feet had wings. Her victim would be lying on the floor inside the window and she'd have to hoist him over her shoulder and then bring him down the ladder.

In a real fire, Gina would have to determine the weight of the victim before deciding which approach to take, but in practice drills, a dummy was usually provided. Evidently not this time!

She spotted her victim lying facedown on the floor as she swung her leg inside the building. First she had to take off his turnout coat and heavy boots to lighten the load.

"Grady!" she cried out in shock as she turned him over. "What's going on?"

"I'm supposed to be unconscious," he replied in a no-nonsense voice. But his eyes were smiling, something she hadn't seen for so long she almost forgot what she was doing. "You're losing precious seconds. Undress me," he whispered in a voice she hadn't heard since that night at the condo. With shaking hands she knelt down and began to unfasten his turnout coat.

"This isn't fair, Grady. I was supposed to be provided with a victim I could manage," she said quietly, easing his arm out of one sleeve with difficulty because she was getting no cooperation from Grady.

"Don't tell me that now, Gina. A fire fighter needs to have confidence that his buddy can get him out of trouble in any situation."

"If this were a real fire, I'd try to get you out even if I died in the process, but a practice drill is something else again."

His eyes narrowed provocatively. "Everyone's going to be watching you, Gina. If you can't bring me down now, I think you can imagine what the guys are going to say."

Her face went beet red. "If I crumple from the weight, we'll both end up in the hospital."

His sudden smile mocked her. "I thought you were the woman willing to take any risks. If I'm game, what's the problem?"

"There's no problem," she whispered, but inside her anxiety had reached its peak. "You'll have to cooperate, Grady, or else this will be terribly dangerous."

"Of course. What do you want me to do?" He appeared to be enjoying himself as she pulled off the other sleeve and turned toward his feet to undo the boots. "I'd like those to stay on, if you don't mind." He moved his feet away.

"But they weigh too much. Besides, you're supposed to be unconscious—so you can't talk back."

"You'll have to do it my way, Gina, or we won't do it at all," he said in a tone that brooked no argument.

She bowed her head as a shudder racked her body. "I'm afraid you'll get hurt, Grady."

"Is that all that's holding you back? Come on, Gina. Where's your sense of adventure?"

His goading drove her to action and she rolled him on his side. Next, she crouched in front of him and placed his arms over her left shoulder, then raised herself on to her left knee with her right foot flat on the floor. She counted to three and started to stand up, clutching him around the thighs, but suddenly she was pushed to the floor, flat on her back. Grady's body covered hers from head to foot. Even through the thick padding of her turnout coat, she could feel the pounding of their hearts.

"You did that on purpose," she cried out, furious with him and far too aware of their closeness.

"That's right." She felt his warm breath against her mouth and she forgot where they were or what they were supposed to be doing. "Never underestimate your victim. He might become uncontrollable, like this." In a lightning move, Grady's mouth descended on hers, and she almost lost consciousness under its driving force. He didn't allow her a breath. He pinned her hands to the floor on either side of her head, and she twisted and turned to elude him.

"Someone will see us!" she cried frantically.

His low chuckle sent chills through her quivering body. "No, they won't. I arranged it so you'd be last up the ladder." Again, his lips covered hers with smothering force and he slowly and expertly began drawing a response from her.

Gina couldn't believe this was happening, that Grady was actually making love to her on the floor of an abandoned building at the fire department's practice site. "Grady," she begged when he gave her a moment's respite, "why are you doing this now?"

His answer was to kiss her again, over and over till she wasn't aware of her surroundings.

"You know what, Gina? You ask too many questions, but this is one I'll answer." He finally lifted his head and stared down at her intently. "I'm going away on a leave of absence, and I'm not at all certain that I'm coming back to Utah. I wanted to see you before I left and this seemed as good a time as any."

"What?" she raised her head from the floor, but he held her down with the pressure of his hands on her shoulders. "Grady—where are you going? Why?" Her eyes searched his for answers but they remained a blank gray.

"You're a fine fire fighter, Gina. After our dive in the river the other day, I realized just how fine. You'll go a long way in the department, because you've made a reputation for yourself already. You can have a secure future here." His hand caressed her chin. "I'm proud of you, Gina, and I happen to know that if I'd cooperated, you would have lifted me down that ladder today. I have no doubts."

Gina's body was racked with fresh pain. "There's no need for you to leave, Grady. I handed in my resignation the other day. I'm moving back to California on the tenth. I should never have come here in the first place. It's disrupted your whole life." Hot tears trickled out of the corners of her eyes. "Please don't go away on my account."

"I'm not," he murmured, sounding very faraway. "I'm going for me. Whether you stay here or move to California is immaterial at this point."

She sensed the finality of his words, and there was nothing more to say. Gina got to her feet and reached for her helmet while Grady shrugged into his turnout coat. He faced her with a look of incredible tenderness shining out of his eyes.' "For old times' sake, I'm going to carry you over the threshold. It won't be exactly the same as in Beirut, but if we don't get back down that ladder, someone's going to come looking for us."

He gave her an almost wistful smile, then softly kissed her lips before hoisting her over his shoulder like so much fluff. With his usual economy of movement, he stepped over the ledge to the cheers of everyone below. His arms held her securely around the thighs and her head bobbed as he descended the ladder. He wasn't even out of breath when they reached the ground.

Gina had to put on the performance of her life, smiling as everyone started in with the comments and the ribbing about who was rescuing whom. Grady still held her in his arms.

"I'm afraid I played a little joke on Ms Lindsay," he explained to anyone listening, "but she took it like a man." The guys laughed and joked with Grady, who stood grinning among his crew.

As he lowered her to the ground their eyes met for a brief moment. His said goodbye. She turned away abruptly, needing to escape before she fell apart.

"Gina? Wait up," Mavis called out. "What happened up there?" She hurried to catch up with Gina, who was walking quickly toward the engine.

"I'll call you later and tell you all about it," Gina shouted over her shoulder. Mavis didn't pursue the issue. She eyed Gina thoughtfully for a moment before walking over to her engine.

"Can we go back to the station, Captain?" Gina asked quietly.

Blaylock gave her a shrewd look and nodded. "Sure. We're just waiting for Marty. Are you okay, Gina?"

She couldn't answer him.

CHAPTER TEN

UNBEKNOWNST TO GINA, Captain Blaylock had planned a surprise dinner in honor of her last night with the station. Someone had gone out to Bountiful to bring her favorite Chinese food from the Mandarin, while the others had decorated the lounge with crepe paper streamers. A huge chocolate cake with chocolate frosting stood in the center of the table. An enormous package was propped on the floor.

Captain Carrera and some of the crew from station 3, as well as Frank and Bob from 1, joined in the festivities. Gina could hardly believe her eyes when she returned from a run to find everyone assembled and all the goodies waiting on the table.

It was growing dark outside by the time they'd eaten. Gina finally unwrapped her gift, anxious to see what on earth was inside something so huge. A beautiful black-and-white stuffed Dalmatian dog appeared as she pulled the paper away. The fireman's mascot. And that wasn't all. An exquisite gold locket hung around its neck on a gold chain. Engraved on the back were the words *You're the best. Stations 1, 3 and 6.*

Gina promptly made a fool of herself and wept, but her tears turned to laughter as those present "roasted" her, leaving out nothing embarrassing, including Grady's lift down the ladder.

At the mention of Grady, she sobered. Neither Bob nor Frank had any idea where their captain had gone. They didn't seem the least bit happy about it. Bob was acting captain in Grady's place. Now that Whittaker was back, he'd taken over engine, and they'd swung in a new guy to cover ladder while Grady was gone.

Grady had told them the same thing he'd told Gina—that he didn't know if he was coming back.

Everyone in the group speculated on the reasons for Grady's sudden departure. Everyone except Captain Blaylock and Gina. She couldn't help but wonder if he'd gone overseas to see about working as a foreign correspondent again. It was the only thing that made sense. Captain Blaylock kept his ideas to himself, but he gazed at her with compassion several times throughout the dinner.

The gong sounded, effectively ending the festivities. "Ladder 1, respond to assist at fire in progress at Hotel Olympus."

"Hotel Olympus!" everyone muttered at once. There'd been talk of reprisals since the building was closed down permanently, shortly after the fire fighters' ball. Some of them had jokingly commented that they wouldn't be surprised if an arsonist set it ablaze to get even. Many businesses in downtown Salt Lake were worried that the closure of the hotel would adversely affect their incomes. Maybe the joking wasn't so farfetched after all.

Frank and Bob got up from the table and each gave Gina a hug, telling her she'd better come back to Salt

Lake to visit soon. Then they hurried out of the station.

In another few seconds the gong sounded again. More stations were called in to assist, including engine 6.

"That's us. Let's go." Leaving everything exactly as it was, Gina hurried out to the bay with the others, jumped into her boots and put on her turnout coat and helmet.

Gina found it incredible that the hotel was billowing black smoke as they pulled up to the fire ground a few minutes later. Every available unit in the city and county had been called in. Not long ago, she'd danced in Grady's arms in this exquisite foyer. Now everything—not just her dreams—was going up in smoke.

"We've got a fire that's fully involved," she heard the battalion chief saying to the captain over the walkie-talkie. The place swarmed with fire fighters.

The captain began giving orders. "Marty, you're nozzle-handler and Gina is leadoff man."

They jumped down from the rig and started pulling the hose forward through the main entrance to the hotel. From what Gina could gather over the radio, an arsonist had started the fire on the mezzanine floor, where the most beautiful and famous rooms of the hotel were located. If it had been on the upper floors the fire wouldn't have been so devastating.

She felt thankful there were no people in the hotel, but it was a showplace and one of the main tourist attractions of the city. There wasn't another hotel like it west of the Mississippi. Gina could have wept to see the intricate cornices and moldings melting in the blaze.

More than a dozen hoses were going at once. When Marty was in place, Gina ran back outside to tell Joe to start the pump.

It was when she reentered the building and started across the marble floor toward Marty that she heard a bloodcurdling scream. *"Gina! Run for cover! Run, Gina!"*

It was Grady! She was so stunned to hear his voice above the chaos of sirens and hoses, she thought she must be dreaming. But some instinct propelled her to obey his anguished cry. She began to run back toward the entrance when she heard the tremendous crash behind her. Instantly waves of shattered crystal sprayed out in all directions. The air was filled with shards of the once magnificent chandelier.

Gina lost her footing and was swept forward through the entry as if she were riding the surf. Without her mask and gloves, she'd have been cut to pieces.

A couple of ambulance crews ran past her to search for victims beneath the twisted, glittering wreckage. "Marty!" she screamed, picking herself up, intent on going in to find him. Captain Blaylock held her fast.

"Easy, Gina. Come on out to the rig. We'll know in a minute how he is."

"Grady's here," she said, sobbing, "and he shouted to me."

"I know." The captain nodded, ushering Gina onto the engine. "He's up on the mezzanine with the ladder. He must have seen the chandelier going."

"H-he saved my life."

"That he did. Now you sit here, Gina, and that's an order. I'm going inside for a minute."

"I'm coming with you. I've got to know about Marty."

She didn't have long to wait. Just as the captain reluctantly agreed to let Gina go in with him, Marty was carted out on a stretcher.

Gina ran over to him and cried even more when Marty gave her a weak smile. "I'm all right, Gina. Just some glass in my leg. Whoever called out to you saved my life, too. I just started running like hell."

"Thank God!" She bent over and kissed his forehead before the ambulance crew took over. As they carried him out to the ambulance, Marty held out a gloved hand.

"Will you call Carol? Let her down easy," Marty pleaded with Gina. "She's terrified something bad will happen to me. You know how to talk to her."

"I'll call her right now." She turned to the driver. "What hospital are you taking him to?"

"L.D.S."

"Captain Blaylock? Could you ask for a police officer to take me back to the station so I can call Marty's wife?"

"That won't be necessary." Gina heard a familiar male voice directly behind her. "I'll drive you."

Gina spun around and stared up at Grady. His blackened face was the most beautiful sight she'd ever seen. "Captain Simpson? Whether I have your permission or not, I'm going to kiss you for saving both of our lives." Gina flung her arms around his neck and pressed her mouth to his, standing on tiptoe to do it.

Miraculously Grady's arms came around her and he lifted her off the ground.

So many emotions were bursting inside Gina, she didn't stop to think who might be watching. This was Grady, warm and vital and alive in her arms, kissing her back, tasting of smoke and soot. Tasting divine . . .

"You came back!" she murmured against his mouth.

"That's right," he whispered. "I flew in from the East Coast a few hours ago. I came to look for you. When I heard about the fire, I drove on over here, knowing I'd find you."

Her body shook with delayed reaction. "If you hadn't come—"

"Don't think about it." He crushed her in his arms, kissing the very life out of her.

Captain Blaylock began clearing his throat. "I think maybe you two better carry on some place else, or you'll find yourselves on the front page of the morning newspaper."

Slowly Grady broke their kiss and let her down gently. "Come on, Gina. Let's get out of here. We need to call Carol and then I want to talk to you."

"Do I have your permiss—"

"You have it," Captain Blaylock broke in with a huge smile.

Grady held Gina's elbow as he ushered her through the maze of hoses and equipment to his car, which was parked next to the ladder. He opened the trunk. "Let's get rid of these." He took off his turnout coat while she took off hers, and they tossed them inside. He helped her into the car, then went around to the driver's side.

Instead of going west, Grady turned north to Second Avenue. "This isn't the way to the station," she said, puzzled.

"I'm taking you home, Gina."

She watched him, studying his unique profile, the way he handled the car as they drove through the avenues to the condo. Her heart was hammering so loudly she was positive he could hear every beat.

By tacit agreement they went upstairs to the lounge and immediately phoned Marty's wife. Grady was all charm and diplomacy on the phone, before he passed it to Gina. Then it was her turn to reassure Carol, who broke down sobbing and said she'd leave for the hospital immediately. Gina told her that she and Grady would come by later.

"Next order of business," Grady stated as Gina replaced the receiver. "Come with me." He took her hand and led her up the stairs to the master bath. "I'm going to take a bath downstairs while you shower up here. Don't be too long."

His manner was mysterious but Gina didn't mind. She didn't want to say or do anything to alter Grady's mood. Maybe this time they could really talk.

"I'll hurry. I promise."

He seemed reluctant to leave her, but finally strode out of the bathroom.

Taking a deep breath, Gina undressed and got into the shower, reveling in the hot water. She washed her hair with Grady's shampoo, loving the smell because it reminded her of him. When she stepped out of the stall a few minutes later, she reached for his striped, toweling robe that hung on the hook behind the door. A sense of déjà vu assailed her.

She wrapped her hair in a towel and left the bathroom. Grady stood in the living room in a clean pair of shorts and T-shirt pouring them each a drink.

"Have a little wine," he suggested, passing her a glass. With only one lamp on, his handsome face was shadowed, yet she caught the slightest tinge of a flush on his cheeks. If she hadn't known better, she'd have said he was nervous, and never in their entire married life had she seen him nervous.

His black curls were still damp from the shower and fell in tendrils over his forehead and around his neck. To Gina, he was the most beautiful man she'd ever known, and never more so than right now, with his gray eyes playing over her face as if he couldn't get enough of her. He tugged on the towel to bring her white-gold hair cascading to her shoulders. Putting down his wineglass, he took the towel in his hands and began drying the strands as if he'd been given a precious task.

Gina felt his touch and it sent shivers of ecstasy through her body. "Grady—" She spoke before it became impossible to do so. "I have a thousand questions to ask, but before I do, I have something to tell you." His hands stopped caressing her hair, but he didn't remove them.

"Until tonight, I felt that if you couldn't tell me the real reason why you didn't want me to work—whether at fire fighting or anything else—then I couldn't accept that and couldn't imagine our marriage succeeding. But now—" her voice broke "—I don't care anymore. If you want me to stay home and wait for you every day, hold you in my arms every night, smell like flowers for you—if that will make you happy, then that's what I want, too. I love you, Grady. Let me be your wife again, and I promise I'll make you the happiest man alive. But please give me another chance to be the kind of mate I should have been in the first place. You're all that's important to me."

His hands slid around her from behind and he kissed the tender nape of her neck. "Gina..." The emotion in that one word caused her to tremble. "I don't deserve you or the sacrifices you've made for me. Come here, sweetheart."

He drew her to the couch, then gently urged her to sit. He remained standing. "I want to tell you everything. It's something I should have done before we were married, but even I didn't know how deeply I'd been affected until it was too late for us." His voice sounded haunted.

"My mother and father were both news reporters working for the same paper. You know that. But what you don't know is that my mother got involved with another reporter on the staff and they had an affair." Gina held herself rigid as the revelations unfolded. "I was caught between my parents. Apparently it was an ugly and bitter divorce. Mother went back East with the man and married him. My father retained custody of me and raised me. I was nine when she left. It was an impressionable, sensitive age, and all I heard from the time she left was that you couldn't trust a woman, let alone a working woman, especially a career woman.''

"Until the day my father died, he warned me to find myself a docile little woman, a homebody, and settle down. Let her know who's boss, he told me. Keep her home, keep her pregnant.'' Grady sighed. "I know it must all sound outrageous to you, but that was the kind of man my father was. He thought my mother would quit her job on the paper when they got married. He was making plenty of money and couldn't understand why she felt the need to work. They argued incessantly.

"After the divorce, my mother came to Salt Lake quite often to visit me, but as I got older, I felt estranged from her and I'm afraid I viewed her through my father's eyes. I'm the reason we stopped having any communication.''

Gina felt sick. She'd had no idea.

"Then I met you,'' he said thickly. "You were the embodiment of all that is sweet and gentle and beautiful. I wanted to be your hero. I wanted to be the kind of husband that my father had envisioned.''

"Oh, Grady—'' Gina hid her face in her hands.

There was a long pause.

"Gina . . . I didn't know how much of my father's bias had rubbed off on me until you insisted on staying on with the department. But it was more than the fear of you getting hurt. I've realized that somewhere deep in my psyche I was afraid you'd fall in love with one of the guys and run off and leave me. That I'd turn out like my father, bitter and alone.''

Gina couldn't stand any more. She jumped up from the couch and threw her arms around him. "Are you still afraid, Grady?" she whispered against his cheek.

"Maybe. That's why I went to see my mother."

Gina closed her eyes tightly. So that was where he'd gone.

"She painted a rather different picture from the one my father had drawn, but what came out of her talk was that my father was too authoritarian for her to live with any longer. She felt caught in a trap. They had no happiness, Gina. That's why she left, and her feelings of guilt over the adultery were so terrible, she didn't fight my father for custody."

Gina drew him closer. "So you found out she really did love you very much."

"Yes." He nodded into her neck. "I'm afraid my father did a lot of damage to her, as well as to me. Now I can see reasons for the way things happened in our lives. That's why I came back."

He lifted his head and grasped Gina by the shoulders. "I know there are no guarantees in this life, but I want you for my wife, Gina. Not the way my father envisioned. I want you to be happy, too. You need your freedom. Talking to Mother made me realize that. You can't put your wife in a box the way my father wanted. It doesn't work like that—but what did he know? It wasn't all his fault. He was raised by Victorian standards and didn't have a clue about a woman's needs. Gina—I'm trying to understand—"

"Are you asking me to marry you, Grady Simpson?" Her violet eyes shimmered as they gazed up at him.

"You know I am, Regina Lindsay. But only on conditions we can both accept. Fair enough?"

"Grady..." she whispered achingly, loving him too much.

"I happen to know Captain Blaylock is retiring in a few weeks. Could you live with me being captain of station 6 and you as one of the crew?"

"Grady!" she shrieked with joy.

"I've done nothing but think for the past week. Barring unforeseen dangers, we should be able to live a long, healthy life at 6. And when the children come, you can decide the number of hours you want. Do you think you could be happy?"

The earnestness of his pleading was Gina's undoing. "I've already told you that just being your wife is all that matters."

He shook his head. "No—that isn't all that matters. I adore you for being willing to sacrifice, but I don't want our life to be like that. I want us to both be fulfilled. If I move to 6, I'll have more time to write free-lance. I still have that urge in my blood."

She gave him her most beguiling smile. "Who knows? Maybe you'll write a bestselling novel about a married couple's life with the fire department. We can retire in luxury."

His smile faded to be replaced by a look of such tenderness, it almost overwhelmed her. "Gina... my mother wants to meet you."

"I want to meet her. I'm thrilled with the idea that you have family. I wanted to get to know her ages ago, but you never offered and I hated to pry."

"Gina, I swear. No more secrets. From here on, we talk over everything, no matter how painful. Agreed?"

"Agreed, my darling." She nestled against him.

His hands played with her hair. "Do you have any idea how utterly desirable you are, standing there in my robe with your hair smelling like sunshine?"

She cocked her head to the side and ran her hands over his broad chest. "I think I'd have a better idea if you showed me."

The devastating smile that always took her breath flashed for her now. "Oh, I'm going to show you all right, but we're not married yet."

"Well, you're the captain." She kissed the end of his nose and moved out of his arms. "Whatever you say goes." She started to laugh at the horrified expression on his face and ran for the stairs.

"You'll pay for that, my lovely," he warned, chasing her up the steps, but he was too late. She'd shut the door and locked it.

"Gina?" He pounded on the door. "Let me in."

"No. I always obey my captain's orders."

"I'm not your captain, I'm your husband," he shouted.

"Not yet, you aren't. Right now you're my fiancé."

"Gina—"

"I want a *white* wedding."

"Don't do this to me," he begged in a hoarse voice.

"And I want you in full dress uniform."

"We'll talk about it when you open the door."

"Absolutely no one looks better than you do in uniform, Grady."

"Well, I'm happy you feel that way, sweetheart. Now open the door."

"What will you do if I open it?"

"That, my love, is for me to know and you to find out."

"I'm frightened, Grady."

There was silence. "Of what? Me?"

"I haven't been married for a long time. What if I'm a big disappointment to you?"

"In what way?"

"What if you decide you like that brunette better than you like me?"

"I thought you'd overcome your jealous tendencies?"

"Well, I haven't."

"What if I told you I've been faithful to you since our divorce?"

The lock clicked and the door opened a crack. Grady helped a little with the palm of his hand. Gina's gaze locked with his. "Is that the truth?"

"Do you even have to ask, Gina? My fate was sealed the first moment I saw you. Come to me, sweetheart. We have so much to make up for."

Gina ran into his arms and gloried in her right to be there. "Someone once told me that if I wanted you back, I'd have to fight fire with fire."

Grady's eyes smoldered. "I'd like to meet that someone and say thank-you, because from now on we're going to be fully involved. Some fires are like that, sweetheart. They're meant to burn forever."

HARLEQUIN
Romance®

Coming Next Month

#3049 ANOTHER TIME, ANOTHER LOVE Anne Beaumont
Laurel Curtis isn't planning to change her status as a single mother. A traumatic experience with one man was enough. Connor Dyson, an Australian property tycoon buying the lease on her flat, has other ideas—like taking over Laurel, too!

#3050 PARTNERS IN PASSION Rosemary Carter
Teri comes back to her grandfather's African game farm where eight years ago, before she had to move with her parents, she had loved Rafe—and thought he loved her, too. Now Rafe greets her as a stranger.

#3051 FACE VALUE Rosemary Hammond
Christine agrees to do one last modeling job before she changes careers. John Falconer, however, has devised the assignment of a commercial for his company simply to meet her—and he offers Chris another proposition entirely.

#3052 HOME FOR LOVE Ellen James
When interior designer Kate Melrose is hired to redecorate an unknown client's home, she falls instantly in love—with the house! But she soon falls even harder for its owner, the handsome, irascible Steven Reid.

#3053 THE CHAIN OF DESTINY Betty Neels
When Guy Bowers-Bentinck comes to her rescue, Suzannah, alone in the world and without a job, is forced to accept his help. Not that she wants to be beholden to such an infuriatingly arrogant man!

#3054 RASH CONTRACT Angela Wells
Karis doesn't welcome the reappearance of Nik Christianides in her life—reawakening tragic memories she's spent years trying to suppress. Now, though, she has to listen to him because he has a way of replacing what she had lost.

Available in May wherever paperback books are sold, or through Harlequin Reader Service:

In the U.S.
901 Fuhrmann Blvd.
P.O. Box 1397
Buffalo, N.Y. 14240-1397

In Canada
P.O. Box 603
Fort Erie, Ontario
L2A 5X3

You'll flip . . . your pages won't!
Read paperbacks *hands-free* with

Book Mate • I

The perfect "mate" for all your romance paperbacks

**Traveling • Vacationing • At Work • In Bed • Studying
• Cooking • Eating**

Perfect size for all standard paperbacks, this wonderful invention makes reading a pure pleasure! Ingenious design holds paperback books OPEN and FLAT so even wind can't ruffle pages — leaves your hands free to do other things. Reinforced, wipe-clean vinyl-covered holder flexes to let you turn pages without undoing the strap . . . supports paperbacks so well, they have the strength of hardcovers!

Pages turn WITHOUT opening the strap

SEE-THROUGH STRAP

Reinforced back stays flat

Built in bookmark

BOOK MARK

BACK COVER HOLDING STRIP

10 x 7¼ opened
Snaps closed for easy carrying. too